The Heart Line

The Heart Line

A Novel

Hollis T. Miller

Copyright © 2021 by Hollis T. Miller
hollisTmiller.com

All rights reserved

.

ISBN: 978-1-7372241-0-5 | eBook ISBN: 978-1-7372241-1-2

Cover design and illustration by Katie Chambers

The Heart Line is a work of fiction. Names, characters, places, and incidents are the product of the author's imagination or are used fictitiously. Any resemblance to actual persons, living or dead, or events is entirely coincidental.

For K & A

Above all, you must illumine your own soul with its profundities and its shallows, and its vanities and its generosities, and say what your beauty means to you or your plainness . . .

Virginia Woolf, *A Room of One's Own*

One

Kay lay on her back, squeezed the pillow around her head, and took slow, deep breaths. It was 5:00 a.m., an hour before her alarm was set to go off. Her body should have been relaxed, her mind at rest, and her spirit on its nightly jaunt through the heavens. Instead, she was trying to block out the ecstatic symphony of her neighbor, Charlene. Kay wasn't the type to hold an orgasm against anyone, but the volume and frequency of Charlene's euphoric screams were costing her precious sleep.

They shared a bedroom wall which, the way sound passed through it, might as well have been a linen curtain. The woman had no shame, she knew the walls were paper-thin and everyone in the three-story, six-unit building could hear her. It was like she was trying to prove she knew how to have a good time; she didn't even bother to muffle the sound, put her face in a pillow, whisper, no, she was Mount Vesuvius and there was no holding back that force of nature.

And this had been going on for three weeks, since Charlene had started dating Dido: a thick, dark-haired man who smelled of wood musk and the ocean. When Kay returned from work in the evenings, she would occasionally pass him in the stairwell as he headed to his job—the night shift at the loading docks in Red Hook—and it took serious restraint for her not to say, "Hello, Dildo." He was as reliable as one.

She wished she didn't feel so put out by this early-morning wake up since there certainly wasn't anything to be done about it. She couldn't just broach the subject with typical neighborly etiquette—politely knock on Charlene's door and ask her to please keep it down. It was a frown-and-bear-it situation. Oh well.

She turned on her side and waited. But then there was the sting of the empty space beside her. The space her ex, Rodin, had occupied up until six weeks ago. A slender ache pulsed in her chest, not so much for Rodin as for companionship. She began to make audible sighs, opening her mouth wide, pushing om-like sounds out her throat, then closing her lips and pressing air through them, blubbery like a baby. Repeat. No one would be able to hear her over Charlene, and besides it soothed her.

A few minutes later Charlene's orchestral movement came to a close. Now that Kay was awake, she might as well get up and get ready for work. She slung her legs over the side of the bed, shoulders slumped, head dropped. She resisted the bed's magnetic pull while she waited for an urge to propel her from its edge.

Come on, Kay. Get. Up.

The wood floor was unseasonably cold against her feet. She stood and swayed for a moment before she walked over to her bedroom's floor-to-ceiling windows and pushed back the heavy blackout curtains. Startled at the dreamlike image in front of her, she jiggled her head in disbelief: snow. The flakes fell gracefully like tiny white flower petals floating on the breeze, bright against

The Heart Line

the dark morning. It was October 5th. Barely fall. She pressed her nose against the cool pane. It fell everywhere.

Don't stick. Please don't stick.

She wasn't ready for the cold, for the long winter. She was from Southern California and before she moved to New York City, winter had been a concept, lovely and distant, of snow without the feeling of cold. A single winter in the City made cold a brutal reality.

How could anyone refute climate change when winter came a week after fall began? It was 2007, the glaciers were melting, coral reefs were dying, the Amazon was on fire, signs so ominous and urgent they seemed impossible to ignore, and yet so many people did. She picked her phone up from the bedside table: 5:37. There was no time to think about the world's problems, she had to figure out what to wear.

The chill outside had already penetrated through the building. She rubbed her arms, opened the door to her closet, and fingered through her clothing so smashed within the narrow space she pulled as if extracting it from a vise. Half of her clothes were lost in there, pushed toward the back wall. She managed to pull out an outfit: gray wool pencil skirt, two-inch-heel knee-high black boots, slightly fitted black silk blouse, cashmere scarf with a red fringe, and a light waist-length jacket.

Her gloves, hat, and floor-length down coat would stay in their storage box under the bed. Sure, it had to be thirty-two degrees to snow, but it wasn't winter yet, and until the rest of the world acknowledged this insanity and took petroleum-fueled vehicles off the market and put an end to carbon emissions once and for all—don't get her started—the seasons seemed arbitrary markers of climate and weather, so she wasn't going to dress up like a snow woman.

She hung her outfit on the top ledge of the bathroom door. It was time to shower, brush teeth, moisturize, dress, and put on her lip gloss, light gray eyeshadow, and mascara—anything more made her small round face look like a clown. She blow-dried her hair and brushed it out with a comb, tugging on the ends; it was a labor of love. At twenty-five years old, she was still attached to her Rapunzel-like hair. Most women in the office wore their hair somewhere between their chin and shoulders, but Kay's hair rested just above her tail bone. Most of the time she wore it up or in a long braid, but today she needed a protective sheath against the cold, so she would wear it down with a clip on each side to keep it from falling across her face. Ambivalent about Preeny's corporate culture and its overreaching norms of conformity, keeping her hair long was her quiet act of defiance.

The wood floors creaked as she walked back to the bedroom. From her dresser she took a pair of gold string earrings and pulled them through her ear lobes. She picked up the bottle of Zen perfume, spritzed her wrists and rubbed them along the sides of her neck—citrus with a touch of floral. She turned toward the floor-length mirror leaning against the nonworking fireplace in the bedroom.

It was never easy for her to take in her reflection, she certainly wasn't unattractive, and there were times when she took note of men and even women noticing her. In their attention she often sensed desire, a desire that was in her as well, though she never quite knew what to do with it; it danced inside of her with titillating possibilities until, unable to take hold of it and direct it, the desire evaporated like smoke, and she was left wondering what she'd missed. In the mirror she felt a dissonance with the image she saw—it could never live up to the image she hoped to present to the world. Her hips looked too hippy, her nose too flat, her skin tone patchy with freckles, her outfit not quite coordinated or in sync with how she imagined herself. And her eyes were far set, which seemed a perfectly acceptable feature, but when she was in grade school Vincent Combs had teased her incessantly about having eyes on the side of her head, told her she looked like a snake, and she'd never been able to completely shake that image of herself.

Then there was the question that always presented itself as she stared into the mirror—*Who are you?*—that she never quite knew how to answer.

Since Rodin left, or rather, since she'd kicked him out, she looked at herself with a new commitment: to accept. Love who you are—a clichéd mantra that practically induced her self-loathing because it made self-love seem like a quick and easy prescription. To Kay though, it seemed the most mysterious and ethereal kind of love. She stood looking at herself and practiced withholding criticism. She looked fine, just fine. The flare of red fringe at the end of her scarf was vibrant and that's how she wanted to feel. Her face, however, didn't look as alive, in it lurked melancholy. The reasons for the melancholy were a thicket she didn't risk approaching for fear it would swallow her whole and she'd never be able to free herself from it. All she could do was quietly acknowledge it was there.

With her hands she smoothed out the folds in her clothes, then pushed her hair behind her shoulders to drape the length of her back. She paused and stared.

Who are you?

She waited. A siren blared from up the street.

No answer came. The exercise was over.

In the kitchen she opened the refrigerator. The smell was sterile, cold and tinny. A Fuji apple half-eaten, it's insides an oxidized caramel brown, sat on the top shelf, along with a quarter loaf of multigrain bread, a jar of peanut butter, Nutella, and last night's leftover chicken marsala from the Red Horse Café. In the side door there was a jar of pepperoncini, a jar of cornichons, and one of sauerkraut. Rodin devoured anything pickled; Kay didn't. She'd been meaning to dump these, but the clock above the stove read 6:47. She closed the refrigerator door. It was time to go.

As soon as she stepped out the front door a wintry gust smacked her face. She thought twice about her decision not to take her hat, gloves, and coat, and cursed the impractical side of vanity. After already making it down the four flights of stairs, she wasn't going back. White snowflakes settled on the arms of her jacket then dissolved. She braced herself and trudged ahead to Seventh Avenue.

Normally, she didn't have to be in until nine o'clock, but a new senior associate, Peter Bowen, had recently transferred from the New Jersey office and asked her for a meeting. It was clear he was anxious to get on a good project and wanted to meet with Kay, his professional development manager as soon as possible. She had suggested 10:00 a.m. following her 9:00 a.m. meeting with her supervisor, Jane Woods. He wrote back and suggested 8:00 a.m. ("The earlier the better!") It reconfirmed her belief that the consultants at Preeny couldn't distinguish between life and work, and they didn't comprehend the necessity of a decent night's sleep. What mattered to all of them was getting ahead and they went about it in a bull-in-a-china-shop manner.

Kay didn't have to accommodate an 8:00 a.m. meeting, but she would. It was New York after all, where people expected more of you than anywhere else.

With no time to make breakfast, she walked into Le Bagel, just around the corner from her apartment. The warm, yeasty

The Heart Line

smell of dough filled the place. It was still early enough that the line was manageable. Buddy, the guy who always made her order, winked at her and with a quick lift of his chin asked, "How you doin' today, Ms. Manning?" He was just about to draw a knife through an everything bagel when she quickly stopped him, "Sesame today, Buddy. Sorry. I have a meeting this morning and I just want to keep it fresh." She circled her hand around her mouth. He chuckled. "Keep it fresh. I gotcha." He had thick lips and ruddy skin, and a horseshoe of stubble hair around the crown of his head. He moved quickly and efficiently, taking out a sesame bagel, then a fried egg from the tray and laying the cheddar on top.

Could she believe this snow? he wanted to know.

No. She couldn't.

She always made an effort to smile at Buddy because he took pleasing his customers seriously, and she wanted him to know she appreciated it.

"You need a bag?" he asked.

Kay nodded.

He placed the egg sandwich, warm and wrapped in wax paper, in a paper bag.

"Napkins?"

"Definitely."

"A cup of coffee?"

"Absolutely."

"I take care of you, don't I, Ms. Manning?"

"You sure do, Buddy."

"You know they're opening another bagel shop on Ninth Street."

"I didn't know. Another Le Bagel?"

"Some other shop."

"Well, I'll only be lining up here."

He winked at her for the second time. "Appreciate that." Six more people came into the shop and huddled in line. A thin layer of condensation formed on the large front window. Kay grabbed the small paper bag with her bagel and coffee. Buddy waved good-bye as she walked out the door back into the cold, past the chic storefronts on Seventh Avenue. These brief interactions uplifted her spirit. The proximity of all the shops, restaurants, cafés, and bodegas in the neighborhood gave her a sense of place she'd never really had. These places had become familiar, along with the faces in them, unlike in Los Angeles, where neighborhoods and commerce were separated by distances that could only be traversed in your car, or more excruciatingly, by bus. The texture of human interaction inhibited by a windshield and the gloss of Hollywood.

Her boots crunched against the grit of the wet sidewalk. Rodin was gone and that was good, even if it didn't feel good. She could easily use their breakup as an excuse to go home to Los Angeles, to forego the winter and the overcrowded streets, and the noise, and the smells, and Charlene's early-morning orgasm alarm clock. But this was also a chance to make a life in this city on her own, where life was so big and loud, and real. And what would she be running home to anyway, not her family, a vortex of unwelcome emotions always threatened to take her under when she was near them. She avoided them whenever she could.

On the Seventh Avenue platform, she frantically moved her free hand up and down her arm for warmth as she waited for the F train. As lucky as she felt to live in her neighborhood, had she been better acquainted with the subway lines when she was looking for an apartment, she would have sought one out near an express line. She knew once she stepped onto the subway she would be perspiring from the hot air the MTA pumped in to keep everyone warm. In the fall and winter, you'd try and dress appropriately for the weather only to feel the need to strip down once you made it on the subway; in the summer, it was the opposite, the cold air would blast the heat from your bones, and you would wish you had brought a parka for the ride. She wiped the wet snow from her face and noticed a rat perched on the lip of the trash can beside her, its long teeth excitedly gnawing into the stale end of a pizza crust. She quickly walked farther down the platform. The first few months in New York she'd been appalled by the rats and how there was no choice but to share public space with them. If it weren't for the long naked tail, she might have been able to fool herself that they were cute like hamsters. Eventually she adapted to their neurotic presence; they were creatures like everyone else, just trying to survive. Still, she was always grateful when the subway doors opened to whisk her away.

Snow. It was all anyone could talk about on the train. New Yorkers generally kept to themselves, but today rather than burrow their noses into their papers and books, or stare out the window or at their feet, they looked at each other; their eyes wide and incredulous, they shook their heads and spoke to each other: "Can you believe this weather? Is this the apocalypse or what?" "I've never seen anything like it." "I'm not ready for this. I'm just not ready for this." "I think we've been *Punk'd*." "I've seen hail the size of golf balls in summer and the sky rain frogs—anything's possible." A low laugh traveled from one end of the car to the other.

She smiled at the unexpected warmth. A *New York Post* headline flashed in her mind, "The Upside of Climate Change: New Yorkers' Cold Exterior Melts." She squeezed into a seat between two passengers who had dressed for the weather—feather-stuffed blimps on either side of her, she did her best to avoid being smothered. Beads of sweat gathered at the base of her ears. Sometimes she missed California. The happy, bright blue sky and the free and easy attitude that accompanied such cheerful weather seemed, since she'd been living in New York, surreal. Although she didn't welcome the snow today, she welcomed the light touch and amusing tone in the conversations she overheard. Taking discreet bites of her bagel, she felt unusually optimistic as she settled in for the hour train ride to Midtown.

Today, for the first time, she thought it might actually be possible to let go of the shame she felt after waking up to the reality of her and Rodin's relationship. When they'd met two years ago in L.A. at Luna's open mic night, she had been completely taken with him. The way he leaned against the bar with a seductive smirk and watched her sing with fervor (as she liked to say) and trembling hands, while her best friend, Maddy, played guitar, made her body temperature rise. He wore black leather pants and a red T-shirt so worn it was almost pink. It was clear she had caught his attention and it made her bold enough to walk up to the bar and sit down next to him. But her boldness stopped there, she was too nervous to start a conversation with him. Hopelessly uninformed about cocktails, she ordered a rum and Coke because it's the only one that came to mind. Normally, she would have ordered beer or wine, but the beer would bloat her, and she thought she'd seem too bougie with a glass of wine. He told the bartender to put her drink on his tab and then ordered a beer for himself. She swallowed her breathlessness.

"You did great up there," he said. "Your voice has a raw quality."

"It's my throat nodules," she said, as if her voice belonged to the nodules and not her.

The Heart Line

"Do you sing at other clubs?" he asked.

For a second, she thought he was teasing her and stared at him a moment too long before she shook her head no. He clinked his beer bottle to her glass. She wasn't sure what they were toasting, or maybe he was just trying to encourage her.

He explained that he was the lead singer in a band called the Corrugators. *What an awful name*, she'd thought.

"I'm an HR analyst," she said, and immediately regretted it because, really, where was that going to lead them? "But I do this on the side," she continued and regretted saying that as well.

He looked at her doubtfully but was gracious enough to smile. Maybe they could practice harmonizing sometime, he said. She gave him a look of worried terror and he started to laugh—his mouth wide and open with perfectly straight, yellow-tinged teeth. What? Didn't she want to harmonize?

She sipped on her rum and Coke and puckered her face at its sweetness while she rotated back and forth on the barstool, her giddiness getting the best of her until he said, "Or we could ride the teacups at Disneyland?" She stopped and let out a large, embarrassed sigh.

"Seriously," he said, "we should get together." She didn't know what he meant exactly—we should sing a song together? We should go out? We should make out? She had a tendency to get hung up on the finer points of communication. And she had a tough time believing he could really be interested in her. "We're playing at the Troubadour in a week," he continued. "Why don't you come?"

He didn't just sing in his garage. *A singer in a real band*, she thought dreamily. A profession she fantasized about, but never had the courage or confidence to pursue beyond the occasional open mic. To Kay, the Troubadour might as well have been the Hollywood Bowl; anything beyond an open mic night seemed an unattainable dream. He drummed his hands against the bar and on the last beat said, "I don't know your name yet."

"Kay. Kay Manning."

"I'm Rodin."

"Like the sculptor?" It had to be a stage name.

"Sure." He shrugged.

"You get asked that all the time."

"I do."

After they'd dated a while, he admitted his actual name was Rob. A name he thought too generic to contain the seed of rock stardom, which she thought was misguided considering his name immediately brought Robert Plant, Bob Dylan, Bob Seger, and Bob Marley to mind.

He leaned into her, and she could feel his electricity. "I'll leave a ticket at will call for you. You'll come right?"

She nodded dumbly.

Maddy walked up to the bar on the other side of Kay. Her large, sleepy eyes scanned back and forth like she was framing a panoramic shot. They rarely settled on one thing, giving her an air of the eternally distracted, yet she was razor-sharp.

"What about my friend Maddy?" she said. "I'd love to bring her along."

Maddy lifted her face, looked from Kay to Rodin and then back to Kay, "Bring me where?"

"Okay. Two tickets," said Rodin. He stood up and extended his hand to Maddy. The gesture impressed Kay with its glossy, professional quality. "Hi, Maddy. Nice playing."

Maddy didn't know what to make of him or his hand and responded cautiously. "He-llo . . . Go where?"

"The Troubadour," he said.

"We'll see you there," Kay said. He tilted his beer bottle at her in salute, then walked over to a table in front of the stage

The Heart Line

where two men and a woman sat. Friends, she supposed. The woman had dyed white-blond hair, the ends purposefully jagged like arrowheads. One of the men had long dark hair with faded sides and wore a button-up shirt with the sleeves rolled up to his shoulders. Cool. These were cool people.

The following week at the Troubadour there were indeed two tickets waiting for her at will call. Maddy came and brought her boyfriend, Casey—shaggy yellow hair and Popeye-sized forearms, he was a set designer and amateur rock climber. Originally from Montana, he always threatened to return there, except at that time Maddy was in law school and had no interest in leaving L.A., and Casey was too in love to leave without her.

The stage lights were low with a blue tint. A fog of smoke gathered at the front of the stage. When Rodin came on, he looked like an underwater apparition. He walked with swagger and confidence, like he belonged there and nowhere else, and everyone was supposed to look at him, and everyone did. And Kay fell in love.

The train stopped in the darkness of the tunnel just before the West Fourth Street stop. An MTA announcement crackled through the speakers, "Ladies and gentlemen: We are being held momentarily by the train's dispatcher. Please be patient." She sunk a little lower into her seat. The MTA trained everyone in the virtues of patience, you signed on for that lesson when you stepped into the car. She'd finished her bagel and one of the feather-stuffed passengers next to her had gotten up only to be replaced by a large man whose hip pressed against Kay's. The way bodies came together in the crowded subway was strangely personal (you were so close to people you could smell and feel their breath, and sometimes their weight, against you) and impersonal (everyone averted their eyes; if they happened to be touching you it couldn't be helped, and so there wasn't any point in saying excuse me or acknowledging the awkwardness).

Five more stops to Rockefeller Center.

She wondered if she'd actually loved Rodin or if she just wanted what he had: a life of his own. He knew he wanted to be a singer and he put all his effort into becoming that. Thirty years old when she met him and still living with his parents, he didn't apologize for it. He was an artist, and if that's what he had to do to survive as an artist, so be it. She loved his focus, his passion. An HR analyst at an architecture firm in downtown L.A., she felt stifled by nine-to-five life, but she didn't think there were many other options.

After work she would go over to Rodin's parents' house in Los Feliz, sit on the mottled rug in their basement and watch him rehearse with the band, sometimes until the wee morning hours. They never did harmonize together. It was his stage. Just being near him and the band made her feel like part of something. He was creative and spontaneous and dedicated, attending shows, talking to musicians, listening obsessively to music, scribbling in notebooks, and when she was with him, she was part of an exclusive club.

A year later, they sat in a booth at the House of Pies on Vermont Avenue when he told her the band was stagnating in L.A. and they needed a new vibe, inspiration. He was disenchanted with his manager. The band needed to evolve. They were thinking about moving to New York City. The Troubadour had been the high point of the band's career. As they both sunk their forks into the large slice of apple pie à la mode between them, he asked, "Do you want to come to New York?"

It was November and the Santa Ana winds had been kicking up, the warm air so dry the rims of Kay's eyes were red with

The Heart Line

irritation. In her mouth, the soft cool of the vanilla ice cream with the apple and cinnamon was heavenly. The slogan "New York City: If You Can Make It Here, You Can Make It Anywhere" chimed in her head.

The disembodied announcement, "This is the Forty-Ninth Street Station: Rockefeller Center," pulled her from the memory. She checked her phone: 7:48. It took at least ten minutes to walk to her building at Fifty-First Street. When the subway doors opened, she stepped into the mass of people, as steady as a slow-moving river, toward the exit. Above ground she disposed of her paper bag and empty coffee cup, then she stopped, as she always did, to take in the Radio City Music Hall sign. The bright pink neon letters were even more dazzling with the snow flurries dancing around them. Nearly a year in New York City and seeing that sign every weekday morning still made her feel as if she were Dorothy walking into OZ.

Two

The elevator doors opened to the eighteenth floor of Preeny and, preoccupied by the snow she was brushing off her clothes, Kay walked out with her head down and didn't notice the young man, who had just walked out of the adjacent elevator, holding a cardboard tray with two coffees. He turned left and she turned right, and BAM! she flew back. Her two-inch heels slipped beneath her, and, as she fell to the floor, she watched milky-brown coffee descend upon her in one great splat at which point she screamed a high-pitched "Ay yai yai!"

She lay on her back, a stupefied turtle, and gasped for air while the man, who had lost the coffees but not his balance, quickly descended on all fours to perform triage. "I am so sorry. Sorry. Are you okay? Can you stand? Did the coffee burn you? Just breathe. It'll be okay." She rolled over and bit at the air to try and refill her lungs. He was patting her back with his hand; she couldn't breathe let alone tell him, *Stop, it's not helping.* She noticed he kept turning his head away from her because—she couldn't believe it—he was suppressing laughter. Her shoulders heaved as her lungs finally drew in a huge breath. He collected the empty cups and reached for some napkins, which had miraculously remained dry, and handed them to her. "Are . . . you . . . okay?" he asked again, his face twisting as he repressed his amusement.

"Are . . . you . . ." her words came out slow and labored, "laughing . . . at me?" she asked, incredulous.

The lights were so bright in the elevator lobby she could barely stand how exposed she felt. The coffee was warm and wet, but it hadn't burned her. The young man's eyes and mouth turned down as he tried to make his face as serious as possible. "No, of course not." But then he just looked and sounded ridiculous and couldn't even fool himself, "Okay," he said, leveling with her, "I don't mean to laugh. It's just that you screamed, 'Ay yai yai!' You know, like a mariachi band or, you know, like Lucille Ball." Was he joking? She hadn't screamed anything.

She waited until her lungs finally felt like they were back in her chest. "I didn't scream that," she said.

"Okay," he said.

"Did I?"

"You did." He was up on his feet again and gave her his hand, which she took and pulled herself up slowly. "I'm sorry, this isn't a laughing matter."

Equal parts of her wanted to laugh and cry. Her tailbone and neck hurt. When she'd fallen, she landed on her hair first, yanking her head back. She combed her fingers through strands of hair drizzled in coffee. It was too early in the day for this. She straightened her back and moved her hips from side to side to check for possible bruises or breaks.

"I'll pay for dry cleaning," he said, "hospital bills, buy you a new outfit." He stood there like a shamed puppy, his brown curly hair brushing the top of his forehead. How had he stayed dry when she looked like she'd just been in a coffee hurricane?

She still couldn't believe she had yelled ay yai yai! She probably would have laughed too.

"I don't think Lucille Ball ever screamed ay yai yai on her show. She danced the tango and sang some duets with Ricky, but no ay yai yai," she said, trying her best to regain some composure and brush off the humiliation. "I watched a lot of *I Love Lucy* reruns growing up."

"Me too," he said, a little too eagerly. "I think you and I might have a lot in common."

She gawked at him. His offbeat charm was kind of charming, but she didn't have time for this banter. "Right," she said. "I'm late for an appointment, and I need to . . . freshen up." She opened her arms wide and they both looked at her coffee-and-milk-soaked clothes. A splattering of milk dotted her cheeks and wisps of her hair were plastered to the side of her face. When he tried to wipe them away, she flinched, and he put his hand in his pants pocket.

"Sorry," he said. "I'm really sorry."

She took a deep breath and really looked at him. He had warm brown eyes, a sharp jaw, and strong yet sloping shoulders. His nose was just off center, he had probably broken it once and let it heal on its own, but it gave him an appealing rugged quality. It wasn't uncommon in an office of eight hundred employees not to know everyone, but where had he been hiding?

Back to your senses, she reprimanded herself.

"It was an accident," she said as she smoothed down her skirt and removed her damp scarf and jacket.

"Can I get you anything? A towel? Band-Aids?" he asked. The warmth in his voice unsettled her.

"I really need to get going," she said. "You could call cleaning to mop up the mess."

The Heart Line

"Done," he said. "Nice to meet you . . . ?"

Her back was already to him. She responded with a raised, backward hand-wave good-bye as she limped toward the bathroom. She checked her watch: ten past eight. *So much for being on time*, she thought, followed by *Ugh* when she assessed her reflection in the bathroom mirror. Perfumed with espresso, her strawberry hair lay damp and flat against her head, and although she did her best to clean off her clothes, she had limited success removing the milky substance from her skirt and would need to use her lunch hour to buy something to wear. Under her desk she had three pairs of shoes, but no extra clothes. She brushed her hair, reapplied lip-gloss, and then walked out of the bathroom door toward her office. When she rounded the corner, she stopped. "You're Peter Bowen?" The coffee man, as he was now branded in her mind, stood in front of her office.

"Guilty," he said, and bit his lip. God he was cute, and as soon as she thought it, she pushed it out of her mind. *Stay focused*. This was work, she was professional, and he had just doused her with cappuccinos.

"You certainly are," she said, and cringed at her flirtatious tone. What a morning, everything was off: disruptive orgasms, snow, the persistent and nagging memory of Rodin, flying coffee, her tailbone was probably bruised, and this man was seducing her without even trying. Did she have any control over her life?

The first order of business was to get him staffed, get him on a project in Omaha, or St. Louis, anywhere but New York so she wouldn't have to see him for at least three months, and would consequently forget about this morning's embarrassment, continue to mourn and reflect on her relationship with Rodin (she figured she had a few more months of this in her), and squelch the desire that was spreading like a brush fire in her belly. An enticing distraction: a sign she was alive, but she was a cautious creature, and distractions could breed mayhem if taken too far. She'd been too long without the touch of a man, that's all this was about.

She walked into her office. He stepped in behind her and said, "You know, one of those coffees was actually for you."

"Okay," she said. "Thank you?"

"No, no," he said, and looked at the carpet, and shook his head. "I didn't mean that. I keep sticking my foot in it. Sorry." There was a thread of humility in him, a quality she rarely encountered, and it bothered her. She didn't want to like anything about him.

"Listen," she said, "let's leave the coffee fiasco behind us." She opened her hand toward a chair. "Please, take a seat." Control and leadership were paramount to establishing a professional relationship, which had been jeopardized by this small incident, so she did her best to shift her tone and focus. "You need to get on a project."

They spent the next forty minutes talking about his skills and background: He'd studied biology and mathematics at Harvard and, after graduating, opted for his MBA instead of medical school. In the New Jersey office he was always staffed on pharmaceutical projects for the big companies: J&J, Merck, and Bausch & Lomb. He transferred to the New York office to shift his industry focus and was hoping, with Kay's help, to get involved with the Media & Entertainment practice, have more time interacting with the actual clients, and less time behind the scenes crunching data. Kay wriggled in her seat. Media & Entertainment projects were mostly based in New York.

The whole time he spoke, she took notes and avoided eye contact. In the brief instances that their eyes did meet, a thousand wings fluttered inside of her and she looked down immediately. An uncanny warmth surged through her entire body and she couldn't remember if she'd put on deodorant this morning. A subtle sniff to detect any odor coming from her yielded no results, so to be safe she squeezed her arms against her sides. And was she imagining it, or were his cheeks flush? Whatever was subconsciously going on between them, they both ignored it. He kept talking and confided that he knew client interaction was key to moving up in the firm. In six months, he would be up for promotion and needed to make the time count: Would she please help him find the right projects?

It wasn't completely up to her. There was a whole team of support staff, partners, and ultimately politics and luck that would dictate where he would end up. She encouraged him to schedule meetings with some of the M&E partners and express his interest in the practice. "And I'll do my best to get you on one of their projects," she said.

Before he left her office, he turned to her and told her how much he appreciated her making time for an early-morning meeting. He explained how he had scheduled his dentist and doctors' appointments, and everything else that gets pushed aside when staffed on a project, for this week, and it had severely limited his availability. With her most composed and resolute face, she said, "You're welcome." Then she sat back down at her desk and marveled at her light-headedness.

Three

Peter Bowen arrived home to his Murray Hill apartment at 7:30 p.m. and leaned back into the gray mid-century couch his girlfriend, Sarah, had convinced him to purchase two months ago for four thousand dollars. According to Sarah, the couch was a critical piece of furniture, symbolic of the stylish, warm, welcoming aura she envisioned them creating together. His old, dilapidated black couch with arms as big as elephant legs did not measure up to Sarah's standards; she claimed it was not only ugly, but it screamed single guy, and now that they were living together, she would not allow him to weigh her down with his prosaic taste, and in New York no less, where taste was critical to establishing one's social status. He didn't exactly disagree with her assessment of his couch, though he was inclined to argue that spending their money on high-design items could very well be the thing that would deplete their funds and prevent them from entering the social circles they aspired to. She hardly found this threatening, since she'd grown up in such circles.

Shortly after he and Sarah had met, he quickly learned that she was what people referred to as a person of pedigree—she'd gone to the best schools, her father was a director at an investment bank as his father was before him, and her mother served as a board member for a variety of charitable foundations. In social situations, Sarah possessed a poise he'd rarely encountered, she appeared so self-assured you would think she had bypassed all the ordinary insecurities of adolescence and young adulthood.

Pedigree. A term he had previously only associated with show dogs took on another dimension entirely when he moved to the East Coast for school. Her taste and conviction about how to live a good life mesmerized him. And she had sought him out, had recognized something in him he had not seen in himself, given him a sense of validation he'd never known he'd craved. It was always so easy to follow her lead because she always knew where she wanted to go. He thrived on the challenge of keeping up with her, even if some days it exhausted him.

But sitting on the couch, he found himself aggravated and obsessing, because the couch wasn't actually warm and welcoming; it was small and stiff, the opposite of comfort. Technically, it wasn't even a couch, it was a settee with *tufted* buttons. When Peter had mentioned he thought they could find something better for the same price, Sarah's eyes became wide and feverish. She claimed the value wasn't determined by its style or size as much as it was by the designer: Florence Knoll. Did she actually think this made any difference to him? The only Florences he knew of were Florence Griffith Joyner and Florence Nightingale.

He understood wealth was built one brick at a time and that it took discipline, something he had more of than Sarah. However, Sarah's happiness was critical to the health of their relationship and a portion of that happiness was wrapped up in acquiring the right objects. She promised that this would be *the* couch. But really, it wouldn't be *the* couch, it would be *the settee*. "We can design our home around it," she'd told him when she circled it in the showroom and glided her hands along its taut gray back like Vanna White. He wasn't fooled. The trends would change, her taste would follow suit, and in five years she'd want to update their living room with a new couch. Instead of arguing, he gave in and crossed his fingers that splurging on designer furniture would not become her pastime. And he put his old beloved couch out on the curb.

They were both working their way up the ladder at their respective companies. Sarah, an editor, was paid the industry standard, which wasn't much, but she was up for a raise at the end of the year. Peter had more room to grow and earn at Preeny, where he was determined to be promoted to project manager, then associate principal, and eventually make partner. He missed the oversize, worn comfort of his old couch yet did his best to let it go as he pressed his back into the firm discomfort of this new one and thought about his future.

Twenty-six years old and the plan for his life lay before him. He had the Ivy League education, the nearly-impossible-to-get-job at Preeny, and from his breast pocket, he removed the custom-made one-and-a-half carat diamond engagement ring in a pavé setting he'd picked up that afternoon from Wholesale Diamonds in the Diamond District.

Considering the cost of the ring, he thought the weight of the box in his hand felt lighter than it should. He'd been putting money aside for nearly two years and had planned on buying the ring from Tiffany's until he went into the store, noted the prices, and immediately walked out. A deep anxiety in his chest, he shook his head at how hopelessly naïve he was. She wanted the blue box, the fairy-tale story, and how could he not give it to

The Heart Line

her? He didn't want their engagement to be marred by any disappointment. He went to the Diamond District to have a ring made and then he went on eBay and bid on a used Tiffany box—"good as new"—for $75. It arrived at work three days ago. Sneaky, sure. Wrong, maybe. On the spectrum of wrongs, it didn't seem *that* wrong, especially when he reasoned that whatever money was not put toward an actual Tiffany ring would go toward a down payment for their first home. And the driving force behind all of it was to make Sarah happy.

She wasn't home yet, and he was grateful, he needed a few moments to himself. He let his head fall against the back edge of the couch and started to laugh at the predicament he now found himself in: The entire day he couldn't stop thinking about Kay Manning. It was ridiculous, and not a real predicament. A beautiful woman had struck him. Big deal. The cascade of strawberry hair against that amber complexion with a constellation of freckles dusting both cheeks, and those bright, hazel-speckled eyes would strike anyone. Her unexpected quirkiness intrigued him; that single scream cast a spell on him. He laughed to himself as he replayed the moment in his mind. There were plenty of beautiful women in New York, though he never had the kind of visceral response he had to Kay. Even her perfume arrested him. Like night-blooming jasmine in the summer evenings, its sweet scent just knocked him out.

Quit it, he told himself. Stop thinking about her.

In the bedroom, he removed the baby blue Tiffany box from the back corner of the single drawer in his nightstand, stuck the ring snugly inside of it, and ignored the buzz of his conscience as he placed the box back in the drawer. On the inside windowsill he noticed the verbena plant they recently bought was wilted. Then he remembered how cold it had been all day with the unexpected snow. He'd never kept a plant alive in his life, and always thought it was some kind of magic beyond sunlight and water when a plant did thrive. His mom had that magic, maybe it was a trait that would blossom in him over time. He moved it to the dresser under the light of the floor lamp to warm it up.

He was going to marry Sarah. It was time. They had been together since college and they wanted the same things: to realize their ambitions, have a family, and live well. Marriage was the built-in expectation of moving in together. He still needed to figure out how he was going to ask her. Everything had to be just so for Sarah. Her meticulousness as an editor transferred to all other aspects of her life. If he didn't get it just right, she'd be offended and think he didn't really care. Unlike him, she was from money and consequently her expectations were high.

Peter had been raised with enough, but most people at Harvard had been raised with more than enough. And while he was there the difference between these two realities became clear: Those with more than enough had an entirely different set of expectations. Life was meant to meet them where they expected to be met because it always had.

Privilege wasn't foreign to Peter. The first part of his life was comfortable and then when he turned twelve his father had a stroke. The erudite and rather awkward UC Berkeley Professor, Dr. Leland Bowen, who knew the answer to any question Peter ever asked, disappeared to be replaced by a Dr. Bowen he didn't recognize. After the stroke, his father could no longer decipher the codes the universe of physics presented him with, nor understand or explain what any of it meant to a class full of bright, expectant students. No longer able to afford private school, Peter's mother enrolled him at the public school, and she took a full-time position there teaching art.

The Heart Line

His ambition to succeed grew in tandem with his avoidance of his father. One day at home, while Peter dutifully did his homework at the end of their long oval dining room table, his father sat in the chair next to him, crossed his hands, turned toward Peter, and with half of his mouth smiling asked, "What planet are you from?" A thin rod of ice grew from just below Peter's heart to his throat. Terrified, he forced himself to look at his father. He hoped it was a rare opportunity to laugh, but as he stared at this man whose black hair was now mostly silver and his face gaunt and covered in uneven patches of stubble, so that he looked like a malnourished animal, and his eyes squinting even though the room was well lit, Peter knew he was serious. After his father's stroke, expectations became synonymous with unhappiness, and he tried not to have any.

When the acceptance letter from Harvard arrived, he cried for the first time since his father's stroke. He was the luckiest kid he knew, and he didn't think twice about going. It was the best and the farthest away.

The front door opened and shut. "Peter?" Sarah called from the living room.

"In the bedroom," he said.

"I've got takeout."

"I'm coming." He stayed on the bed. He needed another minute.

With Sarah it was always take out or eat out. They rarely had time to cook, and the absence of the rituals of a rooted domestic life made him nostalgic for that brief period before he was twelve when his father worked, and his mother was home more; when her cooking filled the house with the rich aroma of the homemade soups, sauces, and roasted meats she prepared. There was the bleached, clean smell of laundry, the simple colorful flowers she displayed in vases throughout the house, and in the backyard a modest patch of soil where she grew vegetables.

Two weeks ago, he called his mom to tell her he was going to ask Sarah to marry him. The line went quiet for a moment. Pensive, she weighed and measured each word a person spoke to her and gave equal attention to what she said in response. "It's such an exciting time in your life, Peter. I'm so happy you found the right person for you. You let me know if you two need any help with the wedding planning."

Always supportive and encouraging, she dealt with her disappointments privately. Of course she said the right thing, but he'd almost hoped she would have told him she was disappointed or even angry, either because she'd only met Sarah a few times and didn't really know her or because her son, whose absence had been so gaping when he left at eighteen, would now definitively tie his fate to the East Coast, not California. He loved her because, sure, she was his mother, but also because she never tried to make him feel guilty, never tried to make him responsible for anything she'd suffered. Sometimes he wished she had.

His childhood home had been full of life. The memories surfaced against his will and it overwhelmed him with sadness how quickly and permanently the brightness and happiness of that time had been extinguished. Why this was all coming up now he couldn't say. Maybe it was cold feet, maybe this next phase of life with Sarah had simply spooked him. Kay was nothing more than a distraction. He had worked so hard and for so long to get ahead, and in taking a breath before the inevitable path before him, a portal had opened, and memories of the bittersweet past surfaced along with the fantasy of an alternate future with a woman he didn't even know. He needed to get control of himself and push ahead, as he always did, into the future.

In the kitchen, he heard Sarah rustling through the paper bags. "Peter!" she called again.

They sat in the kitchen at their two-top 1950s Formica and aluminum table—bought at a consignment shop, along with all their flatware because Sarah also had a practical side and said there was no point investing in prime wedding registry items guests would purchase (when she and Peter *finally* did marry)— and filled their plates with mango salad, pad Thai and chicken curry. They barely spoke a word at the table, which wasn't unusual since Sarah often came home starving and incapable of civil conversation until she ate something. Now, her hunger satiated, she leaned back in her chair and sighed with relief. She combed her fingers through her blond hair, recently dyed since her natural color had begun to darken. "Mom wants us to come up on Friday the twenty-sixth for a dinner party she's having in honor of Dad's birthday." She took another bite of food. "We'd need to leave a few hours early from work to catch the train."

Peter checked his calendar. "The twenty-sixth?"

She nodded.

"There's an office Halloween party that evening," he said.

"A Halloween party?" Her eyes squinted with annoyance. She never tried to hide her disgust.

"Babe, I know it sounds ridiculous, but I've got to show up to these things right now. I'd rather go to your dad's birthday, but this is a whole new office. I need to network with my colleagues."

"Significant others aren't invited?" She twirled rice noodles around her fork.

"They're invited to the holiday party in December, not the in-house Halloween party."

"Fine," she said and put her fork down. "I'll just have to take the train up by myself. Sam and Laura are going to be there, and I'll be all by my lonesome." She turned her mouth down, a caricature of a pout. Her attempt at humor failed to be anything more than just that, an attempt. Sam was Sarah's brother and Laura was her sister-in-law. The fact that they had married six months ago was a source of tension for Sarah, who had been with Peter longer and wasn't engaged yet.

He had let her know early in their relationship that he wouldn't consider marriage until after his midtwenties. Any earlier was absurd. There was scientific evidence that your brain didn't truly mature into an adult brain until twenty-five—that and the divorce rate in this country, a statistic that would give anyone pause. There was no shame in waiting, it reflected a more common-sense approach to life, and most people weren't marrying until their late twenties or early to midthirties these days. He associated the lingering idealism of marriage with his parents' generation. Ideals that, strangely, had a particular hold on Sarah.

Marriage was the key to her happiness.

Her life wouldn't really begin until she was married.

Everything up until marriage was just the prologue.

He turned twenty-six three months ago, and he could sense her agony every day that passed without a ring on her finger and the accompanying magical, mythical question.

She rose from the table and reached for the Chardonnay in the fridge, her manicured fingernails against the bottle looked like a bold and elegant wine advertisement. She wore navy slacks and a cream button-down shirt. The red lipstick as rich and bright as blood on her lips this morning was now faded and patchy. Leaning back into the counter, she sipped the wine from a water glass.

"Maybe you can come up on Saturday and we can spend the weekend at my parents. Some time away from the City would be nice."

"That might work. I just need to wait and see about my staffing. You know how the big projects can eat into the weekend."

She was quiet, then: "Why does work take priority over us?"

He shifted in his seat. When it came to their relationship, she plunged straight into what she thought the problem was, rarely did she circle a topic or really consider its complexities. He didn't want to do this right now, but she wasn't giving him a choice. "It doesn't," he said. "I'm just still at the beginning of my career and there are a lot of demands right now. It won't always be this way."

"You always say that, but you're more committed to work than to anything else."

This seemed unreasonable and unfair, especially since she also put in long hours and talked about becoming managing editor of a magazine someday, as if this wouldn't put extraordinary demands on her. "We just moved in together," he said, "most people consider that a sign of commitment. We just ate dinner, and we have an evening in front of us . . . What's going on?"

Her index finger lifted off her glass and shook accusatorially at him. "Don't do that. Don't make this about me having some issue when you're the one with the issue."

Here we go. He took a deep breath and considered getting the ring out of his nightstand. Just hand it to her. "Here. Marry me," he'd say and the anticlimax of it might just break them.

"What's my issue?" he asked instead because she was dying to tell him.

"Eternity. You think that I'll be here for an eternity waiting for you."

"No. I don't."

"Well, I won't."

"I know. But I'm trying to secure our future. I'm trying to put myself into a stronger position in the company and that takes some sacrifice."

"This is a perennial conversation, and I just don't have the patience for it."

"What would you have me do?" And immediately he regretted asking such a useless question.

"Put us first. Move us to the next step. Or else I don't know what I'll do."

"Threatening me is a great tactic." The anger gathered in his throat and he tried his best to push it down and keep his cool. He counted to himself and stared down at her shoes. Those prissy little ballerina-like slippers with those gold medallions stuck on the front just made him angrier. They were ubiquitous in the City and he wondered if the women who wore them even liked them. He wondered if Sarah even really liked him. What struck him most was the I-don't-care-about-what-you-want-or-feel attitude, I know what I want, so give it to me or else. Like marriage was a commodity he could just hand to her. It was this side of Sarah he always found so difficult to accept: when life wasn't moving at the pace she wanted, when it wasn't giving her what she knew she deserved, she started issuing ultimatums, and any chance to create a mutual understanding between them quickly evaporated.

The glass shook in her hand. "I'm not going to waste my time." Defiant. Unapologetic.

They were both investing their time. They were both still young; they were in agreement about where they were headed.

The Heart Line

"What happened today?" he said.

"Nothing. It snowed. It was just another day. Another day in our thousands of days together and I want something to look forward to."

"You can't force this. I can't understand why you'd want to."

She threw the glass in the sink, shattered it into pieces and shards. Incredible. That was a first and he wasn't sure what to do. He gripped the sides of the table. *If she only knew*, he thought. Her timing to strangle and ruin the future was impeccable. He feared what he might say to her; it would be so easy to destroy everything they'd built so far with a few words. How long was it going to take him to get past this conversation and back to a state where he wanted to ask her to marry him?

He walked into the living room and picked up his coat from the couch, put it on and slammed the front door behind him.

The night was frigid and wet. Patches of snow sat lonely in the crevices of the buildings and in the small squares of soil where trees sprung up from their designated spots in the sidewalk. The cold air cut at his lungs. He usually welcomed the brightness of the city, but tonight he wanted to be alone; he wanted the anonymity of the darkness, yet as usual everything was lit. He passed a restaurant with large picture windows where friends and couples gathered at tables and the bar, heads tilted back laughing, faces leaned in for close conversations. These intimacies, carefree and fluid, seemed unreal to him. He gritted his teeth and then stretched his jaw wide, tried to snap himself free of the tension that had tightened inside of him. He kept walking and made his way to Madison Square Park where the streetlamps were just sparse enough and the large buildings and nightlife at just enough distance to preserve the obscurity of night. He sat on a bench, breathed his warm breath into his hands and rubbed them together. Every day he told her he loved her, and it didn't seem to count for anything.

She was uncompromising in her demands and he refused to give in to an ultimatum and where did that put them? Stuck. She put it all on him, it was all up to him; she was just waiting to say yes. He was caught in the dance of this ancient ritual and didn't know what the next move was. Wind whispered through the trees and he shivered. In a couple of weeks this would blow over, he'd ask her then. And would she feel like an idiot? he wondered. No, probably not.

When he calmed down, he reflected on how insecure she must be feeling. For her, marriage was the ultimate symbol of love and until he put the ring on her finger, she had to bear the intolerable suspicion that he might not love her. He just wished she could admit as much.

When he got into bed that night, she slid over to him. Naked and warm she laid on top of him, put her lips against his, took off his T-shirt and pressed her breasts against his chest. He knew she wasn't really sorry. He tried not to think of all the reasons she rubbed up against him and turned him hard. They were good at this. And so, he surrendered to the pleasure of her breast in his mouth, his teeth scraping her nipple. Her hand moved fast against his cock, and then she slithered down under the sheets and he groaned at the hot, wet pressure of her mouth. He grabbed at her, lifted her off of him and pushed her, face forward, against the headboard.

"You want me now, don't you?" she said. He could hear the smile on her lips, the taunt. As she moaned and clenched the headboard, he spread her legs wider and entered her. He thrust himself deep inside her, again and again. Her high-pitched ecstasy made him thrust harder. The sensation overtook him, rushed and shot through his entire body until he lay limp against her.

He didn't want to move. To return to consciousness meant to be back in the room where she was congratulating herself on her ability to seduce him, to make him succumb to her power. But it was Kay Manning that had taken hold of him. It was Kay he imagined underneath him. He was inside Kay. It was her smooth, warm flesh he felt against his, and he didn't want to wake from the fantasy.

Four

At the end of the day, Kay was at her desk peering at an Excel spreadsheet on her computer with the upcoming projects and profiles of consultants that needed to be staffed. Her eyes were starting to glaze over when Carlos walked into her office at four thirty to insist she join him, Amita, and Nikki—all assistants at Preeny—for drinks in Alphabet City, as far away from Midtown and their bosses as they could get.

Amita, Nikki, and Carlos liked Kay. She was young, pretty, and a good audience when they wanted to gossip and shock someone with their insider stories of Preeny. They trusted her. Kay had always been friendly and chatted with them in the break room. Except on the occasion they needed to have a meeting arranged with one of the partners, most of the consultants rarely acknowledged the assistants' existence. Kay had taken Nikki and Carlos out to lunch after she'd seen them berated by their bosses and that simple kindness was enough to secure their loyalty forever.

She hesitated at the invitation because she had splurged too much on an outfit that afternoon, even though she'd used every ounce of willpower to avoid her dream boutique on Madison Avenue (an outfit there would have required dipping into her savings) and gone to Ann Taylor Loft instead. It was easy to rationalize buying new clothes since she certainly couldn't walk the halls of Preeny with espresso stains from head to toe. Even when she tried to hold tight to her money, every avenue and street in New York was lined with shops filled with bright and shiny things tempting her to let go of it. Saving was a task she'd undertaken in order to go to Cozumel with her best friend, Maddy, in February. The more money she had, the more fun she would have, or so she hoped. Maddy had dubbed this the Screw-Rodin-and-his-Rock-Star-Narcissism-and-Love-Yourself-First trip. It had to be fun. Fun sounded so fun, and she wanted to have more of it.

The outfit hadn't set her back that much. In fact, maybe it was the new clothes—a Paris green merino wool sweater and a black midcalf-length skirt with a slight mermaid flair—or this morning's brief interaction with Peter Bowen, but Kay was feeling desirable. And that desire needed to speak, needed to be seen. It needed to mix with the City and the people in it. She'd made few friends since moving to New York. Her life consisted of work and Rodin, and now just work. As it grew darker earlier in the evenings, she often dreaded opening the door to her empty apartment and worked late hours to avoid that emptiness.

Drinks sounded great, she told Carlos. She'd meet them there after she sent out her staffing recommendations.

Standing in front of the heavy gold-fringed curtain that buffered the draft coming through the door, she scanned the room. The low light made it difficult to distinguish faces. The ebony bar stretched along the right side of the room, and the deep red barstools stood tall like long-stemmed roses. The bottles of alcohol all colorfully lit against the mirrored shelves were as bright and festive as Christmas ornaments. When she heard a ringing high-pitched cackle, she knew it was Nikki's. She pushed through the people ordering drinks and toward the front of the room, where they were seated at a low round table in wide chairs. It reminded her of a place she frequented in college where she and her girlfriends would smoke the hookah and eat kebabs and hummus. Amita spotted Kay, waved her over, and patted a seat with her hand. "Kay! Sit. Sit." Kay greeted each of them with a kiss on the cheek and awkwardly lowered herself into the seat, folding her legs into a sidesaddle position.

"Excuse me! Excuse me!" Carlos yelled over all the chatter at the waitress. "Can we have a—" he looked at Kay, "You want a dirty martini don't you, sweets?" She nodded and smiled. Martinis, gin fizzes, and mojitos had become her default cocktails since moving to New York and made her feel slightly more sophisticated than rum and Coke. "Dirty martini, please. Very dirty, if you know what I mean." Carlos winked at the server and she was off. He had a way of making you feel like you were the only one in a room full of people and Kay appreciated it.

"Live music in a half hour, so we need to get our gab in," said Nikki, who tapped her dark purple nails against a tall, bulbous glass of red wine, "And, ladies, do I have a story."

"Who you callin' a lady?" barked Carlos.

"Oh, shut up, Carlos, you know you all woman at your core."

Carlos smiled wolfishly. "You're right. Who am I kidding? Go on then. All us *ladies* are listening."

"You all know my boss, Ansel A-hole," Nikki continued. Everyone at the table leaned in. "Well, today he has a meeting with whomever from wherever and before the meeting starts, he hands me his laptop and reminds me Tommy in graphic design is working on a presentation for him, and would I please take his computer to Tommy so he can transfer some images from Ansel's computer."

"Duh," said Carlos. "He could have emailed the images."

"Network drive," said Kay.

Amita chimed in, "Most of the older partners are dinosaurs when it comes to technology."

"Mis amores, please." Nikki rolled her eyes. "It's a power trip. He gets pleasure having me at his beck and call." She flitted her hand in front of her like she was shooing away gnats. "Anyway," she continued, "Ansel says Tommy knows which file and just be sure I stay with him while he gets the images and then come right back with his computer. I go down and sit with Tommy and he asks me what file the images are in. 'Hell if I know,' I tell him. 'Ansel said you knew.' 'Okay, okay,' says Tommy. He opens the images folder and clicks around and, I shit you not, it's like he opened the door of some S and M club."

"What!" yelled Amita and Kay.

"I'm telling you there were titties and pussy, cocks and balls, whips and chains popping out of this folder. I ask Tommy if this presentation is for *Penthouse* or something. Of course Tommy's beet red trying to close Pandora's box. But I told him not to bother putting the pussy back in the bag."

"Go, sister, go," said Carlos and gave Nikki a high five.

It always stunned Kay how common these stories of deviance were. "Are you kidding, Nikki? This is a joke, right?"

"Honey, I don't have the imagination nor the time to make this shit up."

"Did you delete the file?" said Kay.

"Hell, no. Are you crazy? That shit is collateral. It's my job security. It's my Christmas fucking bonus. I made a copy of that file. I coolly placed the laptop in front of Ansel during his meeting and left."

"Then what?" said Amita.

"And then he came out of his office, huffin' and puffin' of course, as if *I* had done something wrong. And I told him to shut his mouth. It was no one's fault but his own and if he didn't want his lovely fiancée, Ms. Veronica, or HR to find out about his little fetish, he better damn well pay me some respect."

"This is depressing," said Kay.

"Kay, this is New York, you might as well kiss that wholesomeness good-bye. How can you be so sheltered when you come from L.A.?" said Nikki.

"Give her a break," said Carlos, "Kay's young. She still has a potentially bright future ahead of her and she doesn't need to be sullied by your bitter disillusionment." Carlos patted Kay on the arm and gave Nikki a menacing smile. Kay was curious about *potentially* bright, why not just bright?

"Excuse me, bitch. I ain't bitter. I just see the world for what it is and I'm not going to pretend I don't just to preserve somebody's innocence. Sorry, Kay."

Carlos threw his hands up in the air. "God help us," he said and turned his attention toward the front of the room where a guy had just sat down at the drums and started to tap his drumsticks against the cymbals.

"I'm not *that* innocent. I just can't wrap my mind around it," Kay said, taking a sip of her martini. And why couldn't she wrap her mind around it? she wondered. Subversive behavior *was* everywhere. It had jolted her when she was very young the way it showed up in her own family, and still she believed such behavior was the exception, not the rule. It occurred to her that her innocence didn't slough off as easily as others', and she wasn't sure whether it was willful denial or just her nature to give people the benefit of the doubt.

"What? You can't wrap your mind around porn? It's everywhere," said Nikki. "The problem is Ansel's likely jacking off in his office which is just—what's that word, Amita?"

"Uncouth?"

"Right, uncouth. Downright raunchy. There's a time and place for everything, you know. But if you're putting that shit on your work computer and going to have such a—what's that attitude Amita?"

"Uh . . . cavalier?"

"Right. If he's going to have such a cavalier attitude about it, handing his computer off like that to have anyone clicking around, then he's just begging to be exposed."

"That's what I mean, why would he do it at work? Why would he be so careless?" said Kay.

"Who knows? Who cares? But I'm not about to miss an opportunity to make a partner eat humble pie. They think they're so much better than everybody else, and they're animals just like the rest of us," said Nikki.

"But Ansel can be good to you," Amita claimed. "He remembers your birthday, gets you nice gift certificates at Christmas. He's not *that* bad."

"He gets me those gifts and tries to butter me up because the rest of the year he is *that* bad. You've seen how he talks down to me, or when he can't explode at another partner, because he knows better, and takes it out on me instead. It's like there's nothing else going on in the world except what's happening to him."

"Not all the partners are like that," said Kay.

"No, of course not, and that's why we don't talk about those ones," said Nikki and lifted her wine glass to her lips. The drummer was now pounding full force on the drums while another guy walked out with a guitar to the stage, nothing more than a snug corner in the room.

Kay ordered another martini. Carlos put his arm around Kay. "You all right?"

"I'm fine," she said.

"There are bad eggs everywhere, you know. You just stay good, okay?"

"I'm trying," she said and wondered if coming out was a good idea. The gossip at the center of her conversations with Nikki, Carlos, and Amita was beginning to become depressing. She'd make an early night of it and head home after she finished another martini.

"They just added another consultant to my desk," said Amita. "That makes five. I'm going to quit, I swear."

"You said that when they added number four to your desk," said Carlos.

"I know. I know. It's the golden handcuffs," Amita groaned. "I'm not going to get the same salary and benefits anywhere else."

"You just need them until you finish that degree you're working on and then you can say bye-bye to Preeny," said Carlos opening his hand wide and waving bye-bye.

"It's been years and it's going to take even more years," said Amita. She was in the final leg of a part-time physician's assistant program at Rutgers. She was always working, always studying, and always tired. Sometimes Kay considered going back to school, but she still wasn't clear about what she wanted, and watching the uphill climb Amita was making to change her situation, she wondered if she would be able to muster the strength it took to do the same. She admired Amita and hated to think of her getting discouraged. "It'll be worth it to have a career of your own," she said. "Don't give up." Amita gave her a weak smile.

The drummer pounded away in the corner, and the guitarist was strumming the guitar when Kay noticed a lean man in a jean jacket with a tear in the arm walk towards the mic.

"Shit," said Kay.

"What?" said Amita.

"What?" said Nikki and Carlos.

"Rodin. That's Rodin"

"Rodin? Oh, honey, we've got to take your temperature, that sculptor's been dead for what? A century or more?" Carlos placed his palm on Kay's forehead, and she smacked it away. He leaned over laughing.

"You're so funny. It's my ex." She looked toward the stage and they all looked with her.

"Oh," they all said.

The coincidence startled her, and curiosity kept her in her seat. Although she felt it would be best if she avoided him and left, she just couldn't. He was with a new band; she didn't recognize either of the guys on the drums and guitar. He spoke into the mic, "Thanks for coming out tonight, everyone. We're the Specters." With that he tilted his head back to cue the guitarist and drummer. The music started low and punchy. Kay liked Specters better than Corrugators. No one had come out specifically to listen to their music; everyone was busy in conversation and drinks. When Rodin's voice cut in, it was raspy and intense. His lips curled around the mic in a Billy Idol–like impression. It made her cringe. He closed his eyes. She figured he didn't want to notice all the people who barely noticed him. He hadn't had any great success since moving to New York, and yet it didn't stop a razor-sharp jealousy from lifting its hat. He was still here in New York working away at his dream and she was working away at what? Nothing. Just living, trying to get by.

He may have needed her for a time, but he never really wanted her. Instead of being alone she had chosen to be with someone who tolerated her for fringe benefits and like a starved puppy she had lapped up every bit of indifference he offered her. Even if it hadn't started out that way, it ended up that way. Maddy called it when, before Kay took off for New York, she said, "Be careful you don't become a groupie. You have a life of your own you know." It didn't feel that way, or the life she had didn't interest her much. They'd never had a conversation about what they were to each other. They'd never said I love you. At the time she thought the adventure was enough.

Rodin's voice became increasingly loud, insistent that the crowd listen and acknowledge him. One by one people turned their heads toward his corner of the room. Carlos scooted his chair closer to Kay's and leaned in. "We didn't know about your ex. Bad breakup?"

"You could say that," she said. She did not share her personal life with anyone at work.

The last time she saw Rodin they sat across from each other at dinner on the narrow outside patio of Sotto Voce on Seventh Avenue. In the oppressive August heat, she watched him chew his steak and lodge it in his bottom cheek like it was spit tobacco, while she heard herself rambling—trying to make meaning and connection out of the trivial: *He wouldn't believe how codependent and neurotic her boss could be. Did he miss driving? She was all for public transportation, but the train was stalled for twenty minutes at Jay Street that morning! Did he realize it was cheaper to eat out in New York than to buy groceries (well, not if you wanted to eat at Le Cirque)? Three more months and they will have been in New York a year and two years together.* A void sucked the words out of her. They were a couple, at the same table, yet the way she tried to push conversation and make a connection they may as well have been strangers. A shoulder shrug, an uh-huh, any simple acknowledgement would have helped soothe her. All the hinges she had secured to keep herself together began to squeak. A waitress refilled their water glasses and for the first time that night Rodin looked up and smiled, but at the waitress, not at Kay. The truth was a fist twisting in her gut. He was the void sitting there with his dark, still eyes and his flat disinterested face, offering up nothing, absolutely nothing. She stood abruptly and her leg hit the edge of the table. The water quivered in its glass. A hot breeze lifted the wisps of hair around her face, and gave her the courage to say, "You get the bill." Then she walked away.

At home, she gathered his things in one large black trash bag and placed it on the stoop with a note: *Rodin, good-bye forever.* He didn't come up to the apartment to say, "What the hell?" nor call to inquire what was going on. The next morning the bag was gone, which only confirmed that he had lacked the courage to end it and had just waited it out until she did. She'd been a free meal ticket. She secured the nine-to-five job. She paid the rent. She paid the bills. He was so cool, and she always thought of herself as so ordinary, and lucky to be with him.

Carlos examined Rodin suspiciously and then leaned back toward Kay. "He sings okay, has a certain something, but he's got nothing on you. You a bright light, sister, and he's a flickering flame. He's gonna see you and say to himself, *Damn, why couldn't I keep ahold of that beautiful woman.*"

She kissed Carlos on the cheek. She didn't care whether or not he really meant it, he was giving her the support she needed.

By the third song Rodin looked around the room and made eye contact with the patrons. When his eyes fell on her he gave her a huge open mouth smile and a nod. The contrast with the cold and closed face he had worn in their last few months together was unexpected, but he was performing so who's to say the smile was for her.

After five songs the Specters took a break and Rodin ambled toward her table. His chin-length hair hid half of his face, his eyes only became visible when he reached her table and tossed it back.

"Kay. What are the odds?" he said, taking her in as well as everyone else at the table.

Carlos spoke before Kay had the chance, "One in eight million. And you're a very bad boy. What did you do to our Kay-Kay? She's not happy to see you."

Oh no, she thought. Her head rang. "Nice to see you, Rodin," she said, and hoped Carlos's outburst was an anomaly.

"Don't lie to him." Carlos poked at her. "We can all see you're not happy to see him."

No, this was Carlos being Carlos. She beamed a look at him to shut him up then turned her gaze back to Rodin and said, "You'll have to excuse my friend. I informed him you're my ex, and he's very protective."

Rodin's open face turned more sober. "I can respect protective friends. Let's be fair though, you ended it." There was the familiar twisting in her stomach. "I've been meaning to call you," Rodin continued, "but your note was so final." Carlos rolled his eyes. Rodin ignored it and kept focused on Kay.

"That is a coward's response," said Carlos, taking full license to intrude in Kay's life. "If you want to call someone, you call someone. Don't make excuses."

Amita and Nikki were transfixed. Kay spoke under her breath. "Stop it. Please. You're not helping."

The Heart Line

Rodin's face dragged. His eyes gleamed. "What's your name?"

"Carlos."

"Well, Carlos. I didn't come over here to talk to you. And you seem to be making everyone a little uncomfortable. So not to be rude but get lost, will you?"

"Ooh, la, la. You are a little piggy, aren't you?" said Carlos.

"Who the hell is this guy?" Rodin pointed at Carlos and looked at Kay.

She glanced at the ceiling as if help were up there. Carlos stood and although he was shorter than Rodin, he was bigger. His arms were dumbbells, his chest a brick, his hands rocks. "You want to step outside? I can show you who I am."

"Eat me, you fuckin' dick."

"Gladly. Pull that sorry little cock of yours out, a little salt 'n' peppa, and I'll chew it right up. Yum. Yu—"

"Whoa! Enough!" Kay stood and sandwiched herself between them.

Carlos, behind her, whispered. "Liberate yourself. Liberate yourself, Kay."

"Shut up, Carlos. I don't need you to defend me, okay?" A crown of sweat gathered at her hairline. She didn't understand what was happening.

"Finally," said Rodin.

The tension in her broke. "Rodin. Just go. Let's forget the niceties. I'm not ready to talk and be polite. I kind of hate you and I hate how pathetic I was to go out with you for as long as I did. You're a user. We were nothing. For nearly two years, we were nothing and I pretended we were something, and I'm ashamed." Kay's words knocked all the expression out of his face. He was hit, blinking and trying to find his balance.

"That's what I'm talking about," Carlos whispered behind her.

She put her open hand in front of Carlos's face to stop him from saying another word and with her other hand lifted the martini to her lips and finished it in a single drink. After she wiped the edges of her mouth, she looked sternly at Carlos, "I can't stay angry with you for more than a minute, but you are trouble. Totally out of control."

"I do it because I love you," he said, an impish glee in his eyes.

She waved good-bye to Nikki and Amita, both of whom looked baffled like they doubted what they had just seen. Before walking out the door she turned and gave Rodin a final wave good-bye.

Outside a crystalline excitement and disbelief seized her chest. She blew out a plume of breath and watched it dissolve in the cold. She hadn't known how badly she'd wanted to see Rodin again, how she'd wanted to speak out at him. Even though Carlos had acted like a punk, she was strangely grateful he'd ignited the situation, though she'd never let him know that. Who fought like that? They were cats. She'd never seen anything like it before. It was thrilling and frightening.

As she walked the chilled, glistening streets toward the subway she laughed out loud. The low redbrick apartment buildings huddled around her. Tiny white lights hung from a few fire escapes. She walked by two people puffing on their cigarettes outside a restaurant. On an awning above her a Tibetan prayer flag smiled at her, its rainbow colors so clearly hopeful. With each step an age-old sadness, heavy and crooked, loosened inside of her. That adolescent tendency to want those who don't want you and to reject those who do had characterized all of her romantic relationships since high school.

The Heart Line

For the first time there was a stinging desire in her for something real, solid, and true. She didn't know the first thing about how to get it. Could you even go after it, or was it luck? How did love come into a person's a life? It terrified her to think it might never enter hers.

Five

At 4:00 a.m. the next morning Kay's phone rang, and she thought, *I'm going to kill someone*, until she saw Maddy's name light up the screen. During the time Kay had been in New York, Maddy had finished law school, passed the bar exam and then decided she didn't want to become a lawyer. Her boyfriend, Casey, hadn't given up on his campaign to persuade her to move to Montana with him, where his family had a sprawling ranch. Six months after Kay left for New York, Maddy agreed to retreat to Montana until her existential and professional crisis passed.

Kay and Maddy spoke at least twice a week if not more, compared their city and country lives, and bemoaned each other's absence. Kay never refused a call from her.

She sat up, kept her eyes closed, and leaned back into the headboard.

"Are you drunk?" were Kay's slow, heavy first words into the phone.

"No . . . I'm pregnant."

The Heart Line

She opened her eyes and didn't say anything. Checked the phone again. It was Maddy's name on the screen. "Can you repeat that?"

"I'm pregnant."

Yep, that's what she thought she heard. She gathered the comforter close to her chest. "—Congratulations?"

"I'm freaking out, Kay."

"When did you find out?" she said.

"Two minutes ago."

"Are you in the bathroom with a little stick that has a blue plus sign on it?"

"I am."

"That's kind of great. It's just like in the commercials." She didn't know if she was supposed to be consoling or congratulatory and didn't know if there was anything in between she could offer.

"Kay!"

"Sorry. Sorry. I'm just trying—you know, it's early and I'm not sure if this is a dream or not."

"I promise you, it's real."

"Where's Casey?"

"Passed out in bed."

"Is he drunk?"

"Yes . . . Kay!!"

"What? What?"

"Say something!"

"It's four a.m.! Give me a minute." She yawned as wide as a wild animal. Shook her head. Drew the comforter even closer. "How do you feel? Excited? Depressed?"

"Terrified."

"This wasn't planned?"

"Of course it wasn't planned!"

"Okay, Okay. Let me get my bearings . . . are you keeping it?"

Maddy's breath rushed through the phone, deep and loud. "I can't imagine not keeping it. I mean I know that's technically an option, but I've just never thought of it as an option for myself. Once Casey knows, he'll be building a crib and knitting socks."

The night cast its dark blues and grays about her room, shadows on the wall trembled. It was too early in the morning to think. A tiny ball of cells was multiplying inside of Maddy and transforming into a human being. A baby. A baby like the dolls they used to hold and coo at when they were little girls, yet nothing like that, nothing at all like that. Kay's eyes wandered and fixated on an opening in the curtain where she could see the dull yellow halo of the streetlamp across the way, the skeletal branch of a tree reached toward its light.

"I guess you're having a baby, then," she said.

Maddy finally said, "What do I do now?"

"Go to the doctor. Don't drink any alcohol or coffee. No sushi. I don't think you're supposed to eat cold cuts either."

"Really?"

"I think so. That's what I remember from when my mom was pregnant. How far along are you?"

"Two months maybe . . . three. I've never been good about keeping track." She sounded helpless. "I'm sorry for calling you so early, I just couldn't keep it in and who else was I going to call at this hour?"

Kay shook her head still incredulous at the news. "Are you kidding?" she said, "I'm honored. Besides it's better than being woken up by Charlene's orgasms, which you can hear in real time and full force if you want to chat for another hour."

Maddy laughed. "I'll pass. I'm afraid I'll get so jealous it'll poison the baby."

The Heart Line

"I'm pretty jealous of her orgasms myself . . . wait, your baby isn't the result of passionate, orgasmic sex?"

"I didn't mean that."

"You didn't?" A three-second silence ensued. "What did you mean?"

"Don't read into it. Do you have any news?" said Maddy. "Any news to distract me from mine?"

Kay could have pushed it, demanded a confession about what was going on with her and Casey, but decided to take her friend's cue and leave it alone. "Nothing compares to yours," she said. "But it did snow today, and I ran into Rodin."

"Really? Snow in October and Rodin—that is news."

"It's completely over with him. I don't even know what *it* was. Did he ever refer to me as his girlfriend? I can't recall."

"He asked you to move with him to New York, of course you were his girlfriend."

"More like a free ride." A fury started to churn inside of her at the thought of it. "I don't want to talk about it. Besides, I met a really handsome guy at work."

"A handsome corporate guy? No rock star? No poet?"

"Just a handsome corporate guy."

"Well, this sounds serious. A budding romance?"

"Noooo. He's a distraction, someone to think about for a week and then forget. I shouldn't have mentioned him. No office romances permitted."

"Why do you always have to be such a good girl? You don't always have to follow the rule book, you know. Break out."

Kay could hear the smile spread across Maddy's face. Break out. Free yourself. Why was this the theme of the last twenty-four hours? Was she so inhibited? The light in her bedroom had changed, the shadows grew fainter and disappeared into the walls.

"Maybe you have a point, but all I can think about now is your baby."

"I know, me too. I wonder if it's a boy or a girl."

"Do you care?"

"I don't think so. I just want it to be healthy and loved."

"That's a good thing to want." Healthy and loved. Isn't that what we all needed for an auspicious beginning to our lives?

Six

It was just lunch, Peter rationalized. A necessary diplomatic act to reestablish the balance between him and his professional development manager. Thinking of her as his PDM maintained a professional boundary, at least he liked to think so. He couldn't keep PDM in his mind when the single syllable of her name continued to ping him as quickly and persistently as a pinball—K-K-Kay, K-K-Kay, Kay. The awareness that he was being obstinate and naïve should have been enough to dissipate her power over him. But whatever had taken hold of him had a life of its own and he couldn't control it. It was a problem to be solved obliquely rather than head-on. He cleared his throat and took a breath to center himself before he opened the door to the small French bistro on Fifty-Fifth Street where she said she'd meet him. PDM. PDM. He chuckled to himself before quick glances from the seated patrons shut him up.

The bistro was on the basement level and smelled of garlic, fresh bread, and wood. The size of a large living room with a bar tucked into the far left corner, it was cozy with two-person tabletops along each side of the room, leaving a slim path for the servers to dance between tables. She wasn't there yet. A server wrote down Peter's name and asked him to wait outside until a table was available.

He leaned against an iron railing and tried to stay out of the way of passersby. The sunlight hit the tops of the buildings and he wished it would extend its warmth down to the street. There was so much shadow in New York, even at midday. The City always kept secrets, hiding itself and creating labyrinths with light and its absence.

If only they'd seat him before she arrived, then he could avoid the awkwardness of them standing and waiting on the street together. He knew she didn't want to get involved with him, probably for professional reasons. The office policy was clearly articulated in his new-hire packet: "Dating colleagues is prohibited and may result in termination." But really, who had the right to determine whom a person could or couldn't date? This wasn't the royal family, they weren't children, and the company ought to trust their employees—adults who value their position—to be discreet and professional instead of asserting parental authority.

It didn't really make a difference to him. He didn't want to get involved with her anyway. His objective today was to exorcise this obsession from his system, which had sprouted and spread like a virus overnight. Then he could get back to living the life he had planned for himself, the life that was waiting for him with Sarah.

This morning when he showed up at Kay's office, she dismissed his invitation to lunch. He had lingered in the doorway waiting for a response. Mesmerized by something on her computer screen, she scarcely glanced at him when she said with distracted gentleness, "Didn't we agree to drop this? I don't need an extended apology. Really."

The Heart Line

He hadn't anticipated how easily she would brush him off, and he didn't like it. He tried another tactic. "I can't live with the guilt. I insist you let me take you to lunch."

"I insist you drop it."

He was floored, even though she said it lightly, with a smile and a shine of playfulness in her eyes. He walked right into her office, sat down in the chair opposite hers, looked her in the eye, and said, *"Please."* It was a naked please, sincere and true. He didn't know where it came from.

She blinked and leaned back. "How about La Bonne Soupe at one? I've got a meeting before lunch that usually runs over. If you can get us a table, I'll meet you there."

He had reasoned that asking her to lunch, while a necessary political act, would serve a double purpose and break the spell she had unknowingly cast on him. Powerless against the flawless image his mind and groin had erected of her, the only way to find the flaws and defects was to get to know her. Peter had a number of pet peeves. A land mine of prejudices lay in wait for her inevitable misstep that would blow his fantasy to bits. She'd talk too loud or too fast. Worse, she'd eat quickly, and not chew her food completely. She'd complain about the service, or be grossly insensitive in some way to the waiter; she'd admire her reflection in the silverware or window and exchange glances with other men who would be admiring her; she wouldn't have an opinion about anything, and expect him to hold the conversation; she'd pretend to listen to him, prove herself absent of common sense, and reveal her conceitedness because the beautiful were often corrupted and made shallow by the low expectations others have of them, except to fulfill the inevitable one: to be beautiful.

There was nothing unkind in his actions. She wouldn't know what he was doing and would suffer no adverse effects. He was merely working out a problem, and it was a matter of self-preservation that he solve it.

Securely seated on the booth side of a table when she walked in, want and desire immediately surfaced and pressed against him. These feelings revealed themselves with such urgency at the sight of her, as if she were a magician lifting a black drape from a table of stunning and priceless treasures. He watched her descend the steps, and as her right foot, in a lovely suede heel, hit the floor, he watched her lose her balance and fall sideways into the nearest table where two men were just cutting into their food. Her side struck the back of one of the men's chairs and he jerked forward. Peter's eyes popped, and his mouth dropped open like a caught fish. *Unbelievable*, he thought. He held his breath and watched her recover while she apologized profusely as the man tried to wave away his irritation.

She was crimson.

He couldn't laugh, he just couldn't. It would be the second time in a week at her expense, and he doubted she would ever forgive him. He had to keep that bubbling, buoyant guttural sound from surfacing. He immediately jumped up to pull out her chair and clenched his teeth and scrunched his face up to convey sympathy. She looked at him, bewildered. "So much for graceful entrances . . . ever."

"You make an impression," he said. And they both laughed. The unexpected icebreaker instantly made him feel more comfortable.

She slipped her coat over the chair and he tried not to admire the curves of her body. The brightness in her eyes was even more acute against the lavender scarf around her neck and the silver teardrop earrings swinging in her ears. The feverish color in her face began to fade as she took her seat. "Have you been waiting long?" she asked.

The Heart Line

"No, not long," he said.

They debated over the menu. She recommended the coq au vin and said he couldn't go wrong with the steak frites.

"Wine?" he asked.

"I'll pass," she said.

"Totally inappropriate for an apology lunch, I know."

"Completely appropriate for an apology lunch, but this is also business."

"Does it have to be?" He was straying from his own script.

She laughed and kept her eyes on the menu. "You are dangerous, Peter Bowen. Yes, it has to be."

It has to be. That should have been enough, really. This was business. Go back to Sarah. Get over it. Okay, he'd keep it light and professional. The server filled their water glasses.

"So how did you end up at Preeny?" he asked.

She looked up, considering his question. "Accidentally. I majored in psychology and never thought seriously about a career. Then made the mistake of taking the first job I was offered in HR after college rather than thinking about what I really enjoyed and wanted to do. I moved to New York for an adventure, and here I am." She seemed a little self-conscious like she thought she'd said something wrong. "I'm grateful for my job, but I also want more than just a job."

"You're not alone, I think most people feel that way. We figure it out as we go along," he said.

"I just wish I knew what I wanted to be when I grew up before I actually grew up."

"You know," he said, cocking his head, "I could help you."

Her eyes narrowed, skeptical.

"We here at Preeny are known for our top-notch problem-solving skills. We're world class. Our consultants' brains—after boarding school, an Ivy League education, and management training—are highly valued commodities." He put on his most commercial sounding voice and best shit-eating grin. "We'll approach discovering your life purpose the same way we do mergers and acquisitions. We'll crunch the numbers, get rid of any superfluous overhead that is weighing you down, negative thoughts and such, and then streamline all the inefficiencies between your desires and goals, and finally, lay out the blueprint for your destiny."

She gave him a doubtful smirk. "Why do I think a life purpose may be slightly more complex than M and A?"

"Well it is, but you'll never get a Preeny consultant to admit that."

"You just did."

"Yes, but I'm different."

"Of course you are."

"Is that sarcasm I detect in your tone, Ms. Manning?"

"I'm never sarcastic, Mr. Bowen." Her eyes were so alive.

"I think we've just entered the game of Clue."

The server came by to find them giggling. Peter ordered salad and the steak frites. She ordered French onion soup and a crepe.

"Where are you from?" he asked.

"California," she said.

"You're kidding! I'm from California. What part?"

"Los Angeles area."

"Oh, that's unfortunate. You know the northerners are leading a secession movement."

"I know. They all think they're so intellectually superior and innovative while us southerners are just free-spirited freaks, directionless, and completely lacking in values. And ten times more susceptible to skin cancer. They just can't stand being associated with us."

"You're right. We're total snobs. But that skin cancer thing is true."

A text alert sounded and they both checked their phones. "It's mine," she said. He watched her cheeks change at least three shades of pink while she read the message. When she put her phone away, she looked up with so much light and softness in her face, he felt envious of whomever had elicited such a reaction. The message had clearly altered something in her, but he knew better than to pry.

"Sorry," she said. "My best friend just found out she's four months pregnant and wants me to be the godmother." Her voice rolled with excitement.

"That's reason for celebration. Congrats to your friend—"

"Maddy," she interjected.

"—to Maddy . . . and to you, a future godmother."

"You know, I think I will take that glass of wine. Just one glass." She winked at him.

This was going horribly. She was fantastic. Fragile and shy on the surface, but with teeth to bite and play. They spoke naturally and easily with each other. It wasn't lost on him that being tied to someone else gave him a sense of security and confidence that lifted the burden of trying to impress her.

What the hell was he going to do? He was used to going after what he wanted with single-minded focus. He couldn't pursue her though. He'd do nothing. He'd suffer his obsession because the only way to rid himself of it was to ride the wave to its end. At one point she asked why he'd come to New York. It was his opportunity to be honest and tell her about Sarah, how he and *his girlfriend, soon to be fiancée* had debated between jobs in San Francisco, Chicago, and New York. San Francisco was too close to home for him, Chicago winters too brutal, and New York was the center of the universe for anyone with serious ambition.

It was also close to Sarah's family, which was important to her. Instead, he told Kay how New York just seemed the most natural place to carve out a career.

"You look worried," she said. Her slender, alert eyes caught everything.

"I'm fine. I've really enjoyed our lunch." He placed the last perfectly seasoned fry in his mouth.

"Me too," she said, as if surprised by her enjoyment. "Thank you."

They walked back to the office together. The wind was brisk, and he wished he could put his arm around her. The sun played its usual dance, appearing and disappearing between buildings. It weaved between them as they kept in step with the New Yorkers headed so purposefully to wherever they were going. Just before they walked into the tower of glass that housed Preeny's offices, she told him her meeting before lunch had been a staffing meeting, and he was now officially on a media project based in New York. The New Jersey office partners had spoken so highly of him he was being given the project manager role. She would email him the details. It was more than he'd hoped for. He was sincerely grateful and told her so.

"Then why do you look so sad?" she said.

Her directness hinted at an intimacy between them. He wanted to tell her the truth. He knew that he had already misled her, that she felt something just as he did, and he knew disappointing her was inevitable. It would have been inappropriate to confess his feelings, so he said: "This is just how I look after I've stuffed myself with French food."

Her face was flush from the single glass of wine she'd drunk, but he could still see her disappointment. How strange that she expected an honest answer from him and knew that he wasn't giving one. All he was losing, he reasoned, was a fantasy, imagined potential. Sure, she was great, but she was also new and unknown, which for the moment meant uncomplicated. As quickly as he had come toward her, he retreated. The circumstances demanded it. It didn't matter what he felt. He ignored the swill of nausea in his gut. He was on a project now. They wouldn't need to see each other for a couple of months. They just needed to get inside and part ways, but his legs were still and heavy, like giant pillars they lodged themselves into the sidewalk and for a brief second panic took his breath and his heart raced. He reached for the door handle like it was an arm to grab and lift him out of the concrete. As soon as he opened it and she passed through, he followed behind her and the panic lifted.

Seven

The connection between she and Peter was practically visible, electric the way his attention and interest turned a switch on inside of her. It made her think of the movies, of the fantastical notions of love at first sight, karmic connections, past lives, synchronicity, the One, and all the clichés of love she guarded herself against because clichés were unoriginal, and she wanted something unscripted. She thought he would pop his head into her office. Or they might run into each other in the elevator or common area. Or he might send an email to let her know how the project was going. Or he might just ask her out. The anticipation made her stomach tumble. Every time someone passed by her office, she looked up expectantly.

A space opened up inside of her when she thought about him. The world suddenly revealed itself with a bright and buoyant *Hello there*. Everything was more: the cold more cold, hot more hot, sweet more sweet, bitter more bitter, yellow more yellow; the city buildings were beautiful, towering, geometric feats; the fall leaves were balls of fire, sidewalks breathed, the wind sang; everything had meaning and purpose, it was all part

The Heart Line

of an orchestra that had been playing forever and she had only just begun to hear it.

Then a week passed without a visit or email from him. The self-doubt, which entered her system like a slow-release poison, bothered her more than the fact that she hadn't heard from him. Were her perceptions and intuition so unreliable? Had she gotten carried away? Lost her head and been duped by infatuation? Perhaps she'd imagined the connection between them. Perhaps he was more afraid to get involved than she was, or his attempt to befriend her was, as she had initially suspected, for professional reasons, and now that he was on a project . . . that was that. He didn't seem like the type to let his political motivations speak so loudly. He didn't seem that brash.

Normally, she would have been angry and chastised herself for being a fool for not maintaining the boundaries of the professional relationship. From the outside though, no boundary had been breached, but inside, vibrant colors burst and bled into each other, the vast inner landscape, dark and unknown, lit up, collapsed and began to reform. It would be ridiculous to adhere to office protocol and miss exploring an entirely new universe, because this feeling was that big and loud, beautiful and mystical. She wanted to take this trip with him, wherever it led her . . . if he'd just show up.

Another week passed and she forced herself to stop wondering about him, to stop hoping he would appear in her office doorway. The colors dimmed. The inner universe she had glimpsed faded back into the dark, shapeless void. She wasn't waiting for anyone anymore.

What she remembered from her psychology textbooks about love was its role in human survival to guarantee the species would continue to mate and survive. In one textbook, love was broken down into a series of chemical reactions: dopamine, serotonin, and oxytocin. Each corresponded to the various stages of lust, attachment, and commitment. She hated clinical explanations, the way they diced life and its mysteries into digestible pieces, and in the process extracted its soul. But maybe that's all this was, the chemical reaction had fired its last breath and now she was cold.

That week she left Preeny each evening by 7:00 p.m. despite protests from her supervisor, Jane Woods, that the only way to get ahead anywhere in New York was to work into the wee hours of the night. Jane did not understand any ambitions that didn't align with her own. This was a job for Kay, not a career, she wasn't deluded about that. She looked cautiously at Jane, who stood in her office doorway with a clenched anxiety that lifted her face off its bones, and said, "It'll be okay, Jane. I always meet my deadlines." And then she silently slipped past her.

The Second Street Café in Brooklyn made Thanksgiving dinner every Tuesday night. She sat at a table for one and perused the Calendar section in the *Village Voice*. To be in one of the most fantastic cities in the world and not take advantage of its cultural education would be a crime and, so far, she was guilty. She took a pen from her purse, circled plays and concerts and planned to make plans.

Eating out alone was a deliberate act of courage. She avoided glances from the other diners, all of whom were coupled or with an intimate group of friends, and whose eyes, when they fell on her, seemed a mix of concern and pity. But why should they pity her for being alone? New York was a city where loners could hide out in the open, where anonymity and solitude existed alongside and among the crowds. In a restaurant, though, it was just the table and her with nowhere to hide. The absence of a person sitting across from her was like a spotlight shining on her solitude. Sometimes she had the sense she was enclosed in a sphere of glass. She could see out and people could see in, but sensations of closeness or intimacy, anything cellular—the breath of a person, speaking softly into someone's ear, to give or receive even the slightest touch—were not possible. She felt herself sinking with her thoughts and refocused her eyes on the page in front of her: *Spring Awakening*, music by Duncan Sheik. Really? Duncan Sheik. *I am barely breathing and I can't find the air.* Hmm. The reviews were stellar. She circled it.

When the steaming plate of food arrived, she immersed herself completely into eating every morsel on the plate. On her fork she sandwiched the roasted carrots and beets between slices of moist turkey, then she dragged the bite through creamy mashed potatoes dripping with salty gravy and placed it in her mouth. The sweet and salty on her tongue were a perfect contradiction of flavor. She didn't care if she looked like a ravenous animal. She was hungry.

On the tab she was surprised to find a note: *Would you like to join me for a drink? I get off work at 10:30.* A phone number was scribbled below. For an instant she was completely disoriented. She'd absently ordered her food and barely noticed her server. Had she said anything more to him than, "I'll have the turkey dinner, please"? She spun around in her seat. There he was leaning against the back wall near the busser station: gangly, with sand-colored hair pulled back in a ponytail, a Roman nose, tan khakis, and a pressed white shirt. He raised his eyebrows at her. *Huh.* She reached for one last roll from the breadbasket and took a bite. The soft dough lodged itself like a ball between her throat and chest. She drank some water to get it down. She was curious, but not really interested. She didn't know how to casually walk out of the glass sphere. Besides, going out with this random character who was likely just looking for a one-night stand would only make her feel lonelier.

Later that week she pulled out her guitar from its dust-covered case, and from her bookshelf the *Teach Yourself Guitar* manual she'd purchased years before. She took a chair from the kitchen, placed it in the living room and sat down, pressing her fingers as hard as she could into position. She strummed the chords to "Eleanor Rigby" and when she started to sing her voice was weak, just above a whisper. She didn't want to be like all the lonely people, she didn't want to live in a dream, but she didn't quite know how to wake up either. She made herself cry and then she called Maddy.

For a moment she thought she was in love with someone who might love her back and the two-minute illusion was sensational. It was more satisfying than any relationship she'd ever had.

"How pathetic am I?" she asked Maddy over the phone, as she sat on the inside ledge of her bedroom window and watched two pigeon-doves, seated outside on her air-conditioning unit, groom each other.

"You're human," Maddy told her. "Maybe there is something there, but the timing is off. You don't know him. You don't know what's going on in his life."

She laughed and wiped her eyes with her pajama sleeve. "Why do you always have to be so levelheaded?" she said.

Maddy heaved a sigh. "I live in the middle-of-nowhere Montana with my boyfriend's family and I'm about to have a baby. If I weren't levelheaded, I would go insane."

"Why can't you and Casey just move to New York? You guys could live with me. He'd have no trouble finding work as a set builder on Broadway. Then I could be that loveable, single, yet overbearing auntie who sleeps on the couch, regales you with stories of my dating woes and makes dinner every night to make up for being so annoying. And you would love communing with all the bohemian mothers in Prospect Park."

"Now you just need to stop talking crazy . . . Maybe you should buy a cat or two."

"You think I haven't considered that already? But then I'd be the lonely lady with cats, and I'd rather be the annoying auntie . . . Is our Cozumel trip canceled now that you're having a baby?"

"It is, I'm really sorry. What are you doing for Thanksgiving?"

She had to gulp down a nodule in her throat before she could say, "My mom wants me to come home for Thanksgiving. She asked very politely."

"That's nice. Do you want to go?"

She could hear an edge of hope in Maddy's voice, a silent urging for Kay to have some compassion for her mother. "Not really," said Kay. "Are you inviting me to Montana for Thanksgiving?"

"I was going to, but I don't want to mess up any plans you have to see your mom. I mean that would probably be a good thing for you, right?"

"Um, no. I'm not planning on going. I'm just trying to figure out how to tell her so that she won't take it personally." She glided her fingertip across a thin film of dust on the ledge. The dynamic between Kay and her mom had been strained for years and she accepted that it probably always would be.

"I would love for you to come to Pony. They pluck the turkey right from their backyard—a little horrific, but authentic. It's not Cozumel, but you do get an adventure and me."

It was hard not to feel disappointed about Cozumel. Margaritas, the sun, the beach, dancing salsa, and listening to the musical lilt of Spanish would be replaced by the cold and sparse terrain of Montana. She'd make it to Cozumel, eventually. "I'd much rather spend Thanksgiving with you than in California with my parents and their partners," she said. "How does one get to Pony, Montana? Horse and buggy?"

"Ha ha. We're about fifty miles west of the Bozeman airport."

She'd been acting like a lovesick teenager and felt foolish all of a sudden. "Sorry I'm so self-absorbed. How are you feeling?"

"I'm your best friend," said Maddy, with a tinge of affection and exasperation. "You're allowed to be self-absorbed with me."

"I know. Really though, how are you?"

"Fine."

"What's going on, Maddy?"

"I'm pregnant and living in the middle-of-nowhere Montana with my boyfriend's parents."

"Is that going to be your excuse for everything?"

"Can you think of a better one? Just come for Thanksgiving. We can really talk then."

"Is the baby okay?"

"The baby's fine."

"Casey's not hitting you, is he?"

"Are you out of your mind? You really need to rein in that imagination of yours. Everything is fine. Don't worry."

"All right, but it's a month away. Can't you tell me what's bothering you?"

"I would if I actually knew what's bothering me. Just come out for Thanksgiving."

"Okay. Count me in for plucking turkey feathers."

Eight

The twenty-first floor of Preeny was like a fun house at a state fair. In front of Peter a distortion mirror leaned against the elevator lobby wall and lengthened his body into a beanstalk, a step closer and he became as large and squat as Jabba the Hutt. He rounded the corner into the conference center's main room, an open layout with a communal kitchen where a spread of treats lay on a long kitchen island: candied apples, popcorn, frosted black cat cupcakes, a bucket full of candy, brownies studded with candy corn, and bright orange punch. Then there were the servers passing hot hors d'oeuvres: sliders, pigs in a blanket, chicken skewers, vegetable kebabs.

Paper skeletons hung from the ceiling, the dark silhouette of witches and brooms lined the glass hallways leading in and out of the fishbowl of conference rooms. "Monster Mash" played over the speakers and in one room he noticed consultants gathered around a dance floor; drinks in their hands, they shyly toed its edge. It was early in the evening and they were too sober to step in. The rooms were dim except for the healthy, orange glow from small jack-o'-lanterns sitting on the highboy tables.

Peter's eyes moved back and forth, back and forth, like radar searching for its target. All the support staff seemed to be on hand to manage this circus, but he couldn't see Kay anywhere. He picked up a slider and napkin from a passing tray and headed into a room where there was a bar against the far wall. A beer was exactly what he needed to subdue the havoc of the past three weeks of pressure and sleepless nights. He took down half of it and welcomed the fullness in his stomach.

The clients' expectations were unforgiving and Preeny's managing partner on the project, Dan Cabbot, was even more relentless. Nothing Peter or the other associates and analysts did was good enough. Dan believed that humiliation was the greatest motivator and encouragement was for thin-skinned people who had no business in business. A visionary leader was too much to ask for, Peter knew, but everyone on the team had graduated from the Ivy League, they didn't need a lot of incentive to motivate and work hard. Yet, Dan approached them punitively—he reviewed the team's work at the end of each day and if he didn't like it, he expected them to stay up all night until they got it right. "Make the data tell the story we want to tell the client," Dan said two days ago. And Peter, exhausted, spoke before he could stop himself, "How are we supposed to do that when our data tells the opposite story?"

Dan smiled tightly. "When I say find the data, you find the data."

Peter scanned the room, a person costumed with the head of a flamingo walked by him. He took another drink and wondered if this is how it happened: You give into your boss, you give into your girlfriend, you give into the collective pressure of the world because how else are you ever going to be part of it? The world is bigger and louder than you are, and it doesn't care if you want to come along for the ride or not, it will spin with or without you. You are unremarkable. *God*, he thought, *I'm becoming a cynic.* Then he noticed a line of people inside one of the conference

The Heart Line

rooms. Curious, he walked closer and peered in to see the attraction: A round table draped in a star-covered cloth with a crystal ball in the center. A banner hanging from the table's side read: *Tarot and Astrology Readings by Madam Celestial*. The woman at the table with shell-pink hair, nails that curled like candy canes over the tips of her fingers, and a plush purple wizard's robe was undoubtedly Madam Celestial. Preeny never fell short trying to entertain its consultants. *Absurd*, he thought. Then he stepped in line to have his fortune read.

When it was finally his turn at the table he was taken aback by the movement of her eyes: The left one was unanchored and floated up and around her top lid. The right was singularly focused on him. They made him uneasy, though he thought they lent her an air of authenticity because she had to be nuts. When she told him to ask a question and keep it to himself while she skillfully shuffled the cards (despite her nails), he explained how he had never had his fortune read and didn't really believe in it. She winked at him and said, "Yes, darling, I know. You're all linear thinkers. None of you believe in the tarot or even providence. It's all logic, reason, statistics, but here you all are lined up, anxious as hungry puppies for a reading. Something's awry in Camelot, don't you think?" She tapped the cards against the table and shuffled again. He was so shocked he couldn't speak. She continued, "If you don't want to ask a question how 'bout we see what the cards want to tell you?"

"Fine," he said, resigned to see this through since he had sat down.

She laid three cards facedown on the table then flipped them over one by one: Death—an image of the grim reaper; Seven of Swords—a mischievous character dancing around swords; Three of Swords—a heart pierced by three swords. An ominous reading as far as he could tell and he reconsidered walking away when a figure placing a plate of food and a bottle of water on a small table behind Madam Celestial caught his attention: Kay, in a fringed jean skirt, cowboy hat, and boots. Madam Celestial said something about not taking the death card literally. It meant a symbolic death, a transformation of sorts, a big one, but it would be manageable if he didn't resist the change. "Bend don't break," she said. He nodded, half taking in what she said while his eyes followed Kay. When Kay saw him and walked over, a charge shot up his chest. She bent down and he waited for the murmur in his ear only to discover she'd turned toward Madam Celestial. "Cindy, when you're ready to take a break there's some food on the back table."

"Thank you, sweetie," said Madam Celestial.

As Kay stood up, she looked down at him. "Hi, Peter," she said, and walked away, not even a second glance.

Madam Celestial continued with the reading. "Ooh, the Seven of Swords. Mm-hmm. You're not being very forthright, or someone isn't being forthright with you. Maybe both. But you feel you don't have much choice in the matter. Just be careful, dear, with the death card preceding it, you can't get away with much." She examined the third card and started to click her tongue to the top of her teeth. "Necessary heartache, darling—"

"Will you please stop with the 'darling' stuff," he said, irritated that she, a total stranger, so freely used a term of endearment with him.

Impervious to his agitation, she cupped her hands over his. "Just remember, darling, suffering is a part of life." His vision blurred. His eyes were on the cards; his mind was on Kay. She'd appeared then disappeared. What the hell was he still doing in this seat, listening to this batshit crazy woman? *Go. Go now or it's*

The Heart Line

over. Without warning he jumped up. Madam Celestial's head flew back like she'd been hit by a gust of wind.

In the last thirty minutes, the rooms had crowded with people and the drum of their voices. He scanned over their heads for the cowboy hat. Every person was an obstacle to shoulder past. After he freed himself from a dangling paper skeleton, he circled the floor another three times, but couldn't find her. She was gone. Flustered, his undershirt damp with sweat, he looked out at the dizzying spectacle of his colleagues straining to relax and have fun. He didn't want to socialize. To talk about his project, anybody else's project, what was in the pipeline, what his plans were for the holiday was all mind-numbing. He hadn't come for the circus party; he'd come for her and so it was time to go.

Time to grow up and do what he'd been telling himself to do for the past three weeks: let go of the Kay fantasy, marry Sarah, become an executive, and walk ahead into the life he'd laid out for himself.

The elevator sank to the mezzanine lobby. The doors opened and he stared at the glossy marble floors that, during the work hours, ticked with a multitude of hurried steps, but now only echoed quiet. He walked to the escalator and, as he descended to the ground floor, he heard the tap of shoes at the left exit and saw the back of a woman wearing jeans and a gray peacoat headed for the door. Underneath her newsboy cap flowed a mane of strawberry hair. As she walked into the revolving exit door he didn't hesitate. He crossed the floor, pushed through the doors into the cold and stepped right in line behind her. "Kay." She didn't turn around. He took a breath. "Kay!" She turned, perplexed. She didn't say anything.

"Hi," he said.

"Hi."

You ran after her, you fool, now get it together. "I was looking for you," he said.

"Here I am."

He detected impatience. A couple of suits brushed by them on the sidewalk. "I've been meaning to call you. I just got so busy with the project . . . and I . . ." he stammered, and she watched.

"Once you're staffed there's no need to get in touch unless you're having an issue." Her tone was cool and professional.

"I wanted to call *you*, not my PDM," he said. Her eyes flashed and narrowed as if she was analyzing something particularly offensive on his face. He couldn't think straight. The wind whistled cold through the buildings. Horns honked. He watched cars whisk by up the street on Madison Avenue. "What are you doing now? Would you join me for a drink?"

"I'm tired, Peter. I need to get home."

Peter. It was intimate the way she used his name. He was encouraged. "Oh no you don't. It's eight o'clock. No one goes home by eight in New York City."

"This girl does." And he couldn't believe it when she turned and started to walk away. He was sinking fast, but he'd made up his mind. With his hands in his coat pockets, he stood still and yelled out, "It's a shitty project, Kay! Total crap. What were you thinking putting me with that asshole? I haven't slept in three weeks. I thought you were on my side." He didn't care about making a scene—it was New York City—nobody cared. It was all a scene.

She whipped around. Got right in his face. Opened her mouth to speak and then stopped, and then started again. "I put you on exactly what you asked for, Mr. Bowen. Your request did not include no assholes. And my advice is to get use to them, they're everywhere."

"That sounds like an accusation . . . You think I'm an asshole?"

She pressed her fingertips to her forehead. "What game are you playing?"

"It's the I'm-so-desperate-to-get-your-attention-I'll-piss-you-off-in-hopes-you'll-stop-and-reconsider-my-invitation-to-get-a-drink game." He took a breath. "It works for four-year-olds."

Her partial smile and shaking head seemed to indicate a combination of wonder and worry. "There are better tactics," she said.

"You're absolutely right. But I wasn't lying when I said I hadn't slept for three weeks . . . Do you really think I'm an asshole?"

She sighed. "I don't know you well enough to judge."

"Then we need to get to know each other. So: Will you have a drink with me, Ms. Manning?" She didn't move. "One drink, *please* . . . you've got me begging. My ears are about to fall off out here . . . How about: I would be honored if you would grant me the pleasure of having a drink with me, Ms.—"

She threw her hands up. "All right! Stop. Let's have drinks."

"Let's eat cake!" he shouted. She was laughing now. It wasn't a full-bellied laugh, but he'd take it.

They ducked into the bar across the street and immediately began to thaw in its warmth. Dark red walls and darker wooden beams framed the sunken room. The musty smell of alcohol and wood surrounded them. A few men at the far side of the room had their coats draped on chairs, their shirtsleeves rolled up as they threw darts. Peter and Kay sat at the bar, shoulder-to-shoulder and ordered: another beer for him and an Irish coffee for her. She looked at him and shrugged, "It's my dessert."

"Nothing wrong with an Irish coffee," he said because she seemed to think there might be. Awe and desire weaved between them. They glanced at each other self-consciously, sipped on their drinks, and took in the space and other patrons. Kay's eyes started to glimmer as she relaxed with each exhale.

"Where should we start?" he asked. "Childhood? Adolescence?"

"Psychoanalysis scares me," she said and avoided his eyes while she traced the base of the glass with her fine finger.

"Me too," he said. "I'm just trying to get to know you."

She bit her bottom lip. "I'll tell you a secret."

"I like secrets."

She leaned in. "If a partner ever brings you here for lunch, run."

"Run?"

"This place is known as the guillotine. The place where they tell you 'Thank you very much for or all of your hard work and the sleepless nights, but it's not enough. Time to part ways.'"

"Really?"

"They'll tell you how much they value you, but it's just not the right fit. They'll give you three months to find a job and will even help you find one. It's generous, but it's all to serve Preeny. When you become the CEO of some Fortune Five Hundred company—and you will—you then become Preeny's client."

"Cutthroat and incestuous," he said. "I like it." She drew her head back and eyed him suspiciously. "A joke. A bad, bad joke. This project has destroyed my neural pathways." He pressed his thumbs into his brow.

She nodded. "Sleep deprivation is part of the job. You're all driven to become partners at any cost."

It's the first time someone had framed his career path to him with a negative tone. He'd never considered not becoming a partner. It's what one did. You got on the track and you ran that track, and yes, at any cost. It's what gave you the money, the lifestyle, the American Dream. And most women wanted executives, didn't they? He was unmistakably attracted to her, and consequently the slightest derision from her made him feel grossly inadequate.

"Do you have any siblings?" she asked.

"I am an only child," he said. "Why? Is my lack of social skill obvious?" Letting someone know he was an only child always felt like a confession. It was his strength and weakness, a privilege and curse. Before his father's stroke he had the privilege of his parents' undivided attention and the curse of its pressure. He often felt like he was supposed to grow up faster than he was capable of and remembered wishing he had a sibling or even a dog to play or fight with, or to just commiserate with on occasion.

She bumped her shoulder against his, jostled him from his reverie and put him back in the bar. "I consider myself an only child as well," she said.

"That means you aren't an only child, but you feel like one?"

"I have a half brother. He's twelve years younger than I am—he just started high school. We didn't grow up together." Her parents must have divorced. He resisted asking about it. He didn't want to upset the delicate equilibrium between them.

The side of her face in her palm, she gazed at him, her honest eyes full of knowing were also vulnerable.

"It's lonely, isn't it?" he said.

"It is lonely," she admitted. "At least I had Maddy."

"The pet dog?"

"No!" she laughed. "My best friend. I'm going to be godmother to her child."

"Oh right. I remember now. You've known her your entire life?"

"Since I was six."

"Your BFF."

She nodded. "Didn't you have one growing up?"

"I had friends. No one like that though. No one I ever considered a brother." He recalled his grade school friends as a mass of energy, loud and moving with the coming force of adolescence. A handful of sense impressions: on a back porch discerning breasts in the shapes of the clouds; a crippling charley horse from Jack Ewing after Peter had sent him a plagiarized love note from the seventh-grade goddess, Tricia; sitting around a spinning bottle on the cool floor of someone's garage. Anticipation colored every thought, feeling, and sensation during that time. Peter and his friends were all waiting to become men, which for a twelve-year-old boy meant crossing the most obvious threshold: sex. Never mind that at twelve sex was still a distant reality for them.

He shifted on his stool and looked at Kay in the long mirror behind the bar; she returned his look. When he turned toward her, he pushed the strands of hair in front of her face aside to reveal the smooth length of her neck. "You're beautiful," he said. And right away she looked into her drink. "Thank you," she said. It was as if she didn't know she was beautiful, like it was a secret kept from her, and when she was told it was so she just couldn't believe it. He was accustomed to Sarah's vanity, her constant attention to detail and perfection in her appearance ensured that she always looked good, but often eclipsed her beauty.

The conversation stalled as the intensity between them crystallized. The bar was surprisingly subdued for a Friday night, except for the occasional holler from the men playing darts in

The Heart Line

the back. Midtown *was* subdued compared to the rest of New York—it was about business, not pleasure. Everyone in the bar wore a thick layer of self-consciousness that made it impossible to let go. Then "I've Had the Time of My Life" began to blare from the speakers in the back and two of the men who had been playing darts now appeared drunk as one ran toward the other and leaped in the air for a graceless rendition of Patrick Swayze and Jennifer Grey's iconic *Dirty Dancing* move. It was impossible not to laugh as they tumbled to the floor. Peter shook his head and reminded himself that all self-consciousness could tip into oblivion with the right amount of alcohol.

"Why do they always play such dated music in bars?" he asked.

"Nostalgia can drive a person to drink," she pointed out.

"I'd never thought of that."

She rested her chin in her hand and seemed to contemplate his entire being. Billy Joel's "New York State of Mind" came on and he pointed toward the speakers. "Nostalgia," he said.

"Yeah, but you have to love Billy Joel. He's an icon and this song is iconic." The music spun around them. He couldn't deny how Billy Joel caught that indelible longing for the City with a lyric as simple as catching a Greyhound on the Hudson River line. He wanted to know what music she listened to.

"Alicia Keys, Feist. Radiohead is one of my favorite bands. I recently got the *In Rainbows* album."

"Did you download it for free or did you make a donation?" he asked.

She gave him a sharp, skeptical side-glance as if to let him know his attempt at a character assessment was obvious. "I made a donation."

He hadn't expected any less from her. "You're probably one of the few. I think they're putting way too much faith in their fan base."

"It might not be good business sense, but it's a lovely idea."

He smiled. "It is a lovely idea," and he didn't finish his thought, *and terribly naïve*. Then they talked about the music they listened to growing up. She loved pop and ballads. Annie Lennox, the Counting Crows, Sinead O'Connor, and the Cowboy Junkies had been a few of her favorite artists. He wanted to know how those artists could have done anything for her teenage angst. She let him know she didn't listen to them to alleviate her angst; she listened to wallow in her disillusionment. "I was filled with unrealized romantic ideals," she said.

"Sounds dramatic."

"It was."

His teenage years were all angst, anger, and solitude. He sought refuge in the Red Hot Chili Peppers, the Notorious B.I.G., Nirvana, and Tupac. They found common ground when she started to talk about the music her parents listened to, the music that really made her nostalgic: Tom Petty, Supertramp, Simon & Garfunkel, James Taylor, Joni Mitchell. "All that music just reminds me of my family and the fall from grace," she said. "I can't hold it together when I hear it."

He watched the stress gather on her face when she mentioned her family. He stopped himself from reassuring her it was all going to be okay and urging her not to worry so much, because what did he really know about it? "My parents used to play Supertramp a lot," he said. " 'The Logical Song' has that effect on me." Then he had to know. "What was the fall from grace?"

She launched into a story fit for soap opera. Her parents had been married twelve years when her mother ran into her first

The Heart Line

love from high school. It wasn't hard to see where the story was going. The most disturbing part wasn't the affair that ensued, but rather the way Kay's mother made Kay her confidante and consequently compounded the betrayal against her father. Kay lifted her drink to her lips, and Peter detected a tremor in her hand. "They were over a year into the affair, and she was three months pregnant when she finally told him. I kept breaking out in hives and no one could figure out why. I can't believe my mom couldn't put it together."

"She left your dad?"

"She made it impossible for him to stay. She married Russel and gave birth to their love child—my brother, Jacob. I went to live with my dad. He was completely depressed, and I felt responsible. I stayed at Maddy's whenever I could."

They were both quiet. When Billy Joel came to the end of his serenade the air was a little heavier. She tapped her fingers against the bar and her left foot started to tick a persistent beat. "My dad remarried . . . life goes on. He said he never blamed me, but I blame me." Instinct drew his hand to her knee. He wanted to say the right thing.

"You were a kid. No one should have to go through that. I'm sorry."

She teetered on her stool, confusion and uncertainty stitched between her eyes. "I should be sorry. I don't know why I just told you all of that. It's way too much information."

"It's okay," he reassured her, "your story doesn't scare me."

She gave him a doubtful smile. "It scares me."

He pushed her hair behind her ear and said it again because she needed to hear it, "It doesn't scare me." His desire for her was clear and pointed, but it was more than simple desire. Beneath her thin defensive armor was a rare softness. The fear in her eyes communicated a deep need he couldn't turn away from. She moved him. He kissed her. Her lips full and warm against his and her tongue sweet, his entire body lit up. Robert Palmer's "I Didn't Mean to Turn You On," descended upon them.

"You've got to be kidding me," he said. He took Kay's face in his hands and planted kisses all over it. "I just want you to know, Kay Manning, I mean to turn you on. I really do mean to turn you on." A genuine laugh came out of her, large and loud, it lifted the room. *This is it*, he thought. *She's it*.

Nine

There was the obvious complication: Sarah. Then there was the more subtle complication: how to navigate his conscience and keep his integrity intact while he simultaneously exited one relationship and entered another. He didn't sleep with Kay the night at the bar. He'd wanted to of course, but he couldn't bring her home to the apartment he shared with his girlfriend. And Kay lived in Brooklyn, which meant an hour ride by subway or cab, which in turn meant an hour of sustaining the sexual urgency between them, and though that wouldn't have been a challenge he didn't want to be *that* guy—the guy who, for the sole purpose of getting laid, cavalierly disregarded any suffering he might cause others. So, between kissing Kay at the bar, he paused and asked her if she would like to have dinner with him the next night in her neighborhood. Just dinner.

The following evening, he dressed for dinner and before he left for Brooklyn, he called to check in on Sarah, who was still in Connecticut at her parents'. She asked how the Halloween party went. He made some vague remarks about it serving its purpose and how he had made some contacts. Then he quickly changed the subject and asked, "How was your dad's birthday dinner?" He stood in the middle of their living room and stared at their chic settee while Sarah started in on her mother, Connie. "You'd think she was organizing the Macy's Thanksgiving Day Parade the way she stressed about the dinner." Even though Connie doted on Sarah, she was an endless source of frustration for her. Anytime she visited Sarah in college or since, she always brought gifts of clothes, care packages of homemade cookies, novels, toothbrushes, nail polish, perfume. She was a quintessential mother. Whenever her daughter needed her, and even when she didn't, Connie was there. Connie aimed to please, and she aimed so high and hard at this impossible task that keeping calm was not an option, and consequently those she aimed to please rarely appreciated her.

Peter liked Connie, she always meant well, and when she and Sarah had particularly tense moments Connie would put a hand on Peter's back and whisper to him, "She's so hardheaded. Talk to her. Tell her to stop badgering her mother." He was sympathetic to Connie because Sarah could be harsh, but he was also sympathetic to Sarah because Connie was completely unaware of how she affected the people around her.

"It doesn't make any difference that she had a caterer to do the cooking and serving," Sarah was saying, "or that I made the playlists for her, and picked up the centerpieces. I don't understand what she was so worried about."

"Making it perfect for your dad?" Peter ventured.

"It's pathetic, don't you think? Thirty-two years of marriage and she still wants to make things perfect for him? Just throw a party and be done with it. He'll be happy. And if he's not then he's an ungrateful son of a bitch."

Her vitriol, although not that uncharacteristic, was so close to the surface she seemed unsteady. He sat down on the couch.

The Heart Line

"Babe, are you okay?" he asked. The early-evening sun flooded through the side window of their apartment. He pictured Sarah in her bedroom, sitting on the canopy bed with the lavender and white eyelet comforter. Connie had kept Sarah's room exactly how it had been in high school. Her voice was barely audible when she spoke next, "I just wish you were here." The first pang of guilt since he'd started obsessing about Kay cracked open like an egg. He shifted and stared at the framed photo on their end table of a trip they took with Sarah's family to Nantucket two years earlier: He and Sarah ran hand in hand on the beach. Her hair windblown, their bodies lean and brown, their commercial white smiles unnaturally bright. They looked happy, and they certainly hadn't been unhappy.

"I wish I was there too," he said. It wasn't a complete lie. He wished he could be there for her. He wished he wanted the life they had planned together. Kay was unexpected. With her a part of him he didn't know woke up. It didn't matter that he hated the uncertainty of the unknown, a stronger instinct drove him.

Ten

Kay secured the peach towel around her and wiped the steam from the bathroom mirror. Her skin was dewy with moisture, her eyes bright and awake.

Who are you?

All she heard were the last drips of water falling from the showerhead to the porcelain tub. She tried again.

Who are you?

It came indistinctly. It echoed from within a chamber, distant and wide, a mouth trying to form the words, the sound reverberating until it found its shape:

A woman.

It wasn't enough *and* it was too much. She stared at her reflection and wanted to know: What makes you a woman? What kind of woman are you? What's the archetype? A barrage of names and images flooded her mind: Aphrodite. Marilyn Monroe. Medusa. Hera. Athena. Angela Davis. Gloria Steinem. Hillary Clinton. Maya Angelou. Toni Morrison. Joan Baez. Joan of Arc. Mary Magdalene. Margaret Sanger. These women were bigger than life itself. How did she embody being a woman? What were her details? Why were her own details so unfamiliar to her? At twenty-five years old she still felt the innocent, awestruck girl, who could barely absorb the world and make sense of it, clinging to her. When she looked at herself in the mirror, she saw someone caught between the confidence of womanhood and the insecurity of girlhood.

A woman.

What was she supposed to do with this? It might as well have been the riddle of the Sphinx.

She took a pair of tweezers from the medicine cabinet, leaned toward the mirror and patiently plucked errant hairs jutting from her eyebrows. A rash of red appeared around the delicate surface. She pressed a waxing strip across her upper lip and tore at it; the prick and burn brought her back to the moment. These hairs certainly didn't make her feel like a woman. She hated the darker stiff ones—they were as unsightly and stubborn as weeds. She wished her body was as hairless as a fish, yet she thought she should admire women like Maddy who bore their hair proudly under their armpits. It was a statement: *I won't succumb to the cultural influences that define a woman, I am my own woman, hear me roar, smell my pits, and know I am real. I am a natural woman.* It was bold; however, she was not an admirer of pit hair, chin hair, leg hair, or lip hair, although she had plenty of it to manage. It all had to go, and it would, once she could save up enough for laser hair removal. She wrapped her hair in a towel and walked into the kitchen to grab a few ice cubes from the freezer. In the living room she lay back on her couch and placed them on her agitated skin.

A woman.

She stared at the cracks in the ceiling, hairline fractures that extended from the seam between the brick wall and white plaster. The radiator pipe in the corner began to clank like someone was hitting it with a wrench. The heat was welcome, the racket wasn't. Nothing came easy in New York.

A woman.

She got up and walked across the cool wood floors to her room, where she grabbed a journal and pen from her dresser. She scribbled quickly.

A Woman. Strong. Strong how? Strong spirit. Graceful under pressure. Able to hold herself. Able to make decisions and live with them. Does not give into the pressure to be what others expect her to be. Knows her value. Does not need a man to define who she is. Defines herself. How do we define ourselves? Through our choices, through the actions we take. What choices am I making? Why do I feel so afraid? Why do I feel so fragile?

She put the pen down. She was hopeful. It was the start of an exploration. There was a spirit inside of her speaking, Self to self. She checked the time. He would be here in less than an hour.

They walked along Sixth Street toward Fifth Avenue in Park Slope. Under the trees they passed brownstones; a few of the old gas lamps glowed with flame. Through a basement window Kay saw a family at dinner, a toddler bounced on his father's lap and avoided a forkful of food. Peter took her hand, and she was surprised by how smooth and slender his hand felt around hers.

Al Di La. The Italian restaurant was popular, and didn't take reservations, only the patient and dedicated ended up with a table. Kay gave the hostess her name then she and Peter walked to a bar down the street for a drink, returned an hour later and waited another thirty minutes. By the time they were seated they were in deep conversation about California. Neither one of them had known what a beautiful state they had lived in until they moved east. Growing up, they had each camped and hiked with their families. Kay reminisced about the sparse desert beauty of Joshua Tree. Peter shared memories of Sausalito and how bizarre it had been to walk the rolling green hills

The Heart Line

overlooking the bay to stumble upon World War II bunkers and gun mounts in what was so obviously a natural sanctuary.

When he found out she'd never been to Mendocino he told her he was going to take her. They dipped bread in olive oil and began to make plans.

They'd go in the spring before it was overcrowded with tourists. They'd fly into San Francisco, stay a night and then head north. They'd go wine tasting in the Russian River Valley, and then just drive. The drive would be one of the best parts of the trip. Kay floated above the table; her heart lifted with hope. There was a possible future with this man in front of her. As she floated, he told her about his father. He didn't go into detail—a stroke, everything changed—but the way his face sunk when he spoke made it clear what a painful subject it was.

She sobered a little. Did he tell her to reestablish the equilibrium between their personal histories? I tell you my sad story and you tell me yours, and somewhere in that mess we find each other. We find the buried whole, untouched by experience. Together we become who we were always meant to be, and we live happily ever after. She wished it worked that way and still wasn't entirely sure it didn't. It was a relief to her that he didn't have as idyllic an upbringing as she had imagined. She wanted someone with grit, and it seemed easy lives never produced it.

The gnocchi in cream sauce was silk in her mouth. She savored each bite. They shared a dark chocolate torte for dessert. The bottle of Chianti between them was nearly finished. He'd walk her home and then what? She wanted to invite him up, but that didn't mean she should. She feared too quickly to bed may lead to him losing interest. And she hated that she thought this way. (Did a man ever worry about a woman losing interest if he slept with her right away?) It embarrassed her to be thinking about how to keep him when she barely had him, and how she didn't know how to just choose what she wanted without complicating it with these archaic notions of how to land a man.

Land a man. It was a dated point of view she wanted to deliberately move away from. This idea about strategizing, a game plan to find a mate, instead of trying to establish real intimacy with someone.

Her mind was getting the best of her.

Stop thinking.

After dinner, they stood at the bottom of her building's stoop, their hands all over each other and their mouths locked, her mind started up again.

"Peter," she said between kisses.

"Yes?" he barely took a breath.

"Peter," she said again. His name unsettled her, a gentle shaking at her core. *Don't jump in. Enjoy this feeling. Don't have sex with him. Not tonight. And don't tell yourself it can't be helped. It can. Take your time. Remember, you want something real.* Couldn't she have something real *and* go to bed with him tonight? One didn't preclude the other. The desire was so strong, so pressing. She took his hand and began to lead him up the steps until she felt him pull away.

She turned to face him. "What is it?" she asked. He looked frightened and her first instinct was to comfort him.

"I want to be with you," he said.

She gently lowered her head and raised her eyebrows, "Let's be together then."

He drew her back into his chest and she scarcely heard him say, "Can we take it slow?"

She didn't expect this, nor did she expect the quick anger that rose up and punched at her. He had the restraint she didn't have.

The Heart Line

All of a sudden, she felt exposed. The high cloud she'd been floating on began to sink. "Slow."

"You don't like slow."

"I'm confused is all. Slow didn't seem the pace you were going for." She tried to discard her anger and forced a smile. She wanted to laugh her discomfort away. "I thought you wanted to turn me on. And weren't we just making plans to go to Mendocino in the spring?"

He drew her in closer. "We *are* going to Mendocino. We're going to have great times together."

She glanced up at the light in the archway, moths danced frantically around it.

"I hope you're for real, Peter Bowen."

He pushed the long strands of her hair behind her ears and kissed her once more. "I'm not going anywhere."

It wasn't easy for her to look him in the eye. As much as she felt like she knew him, she began to consider that she didn't know him at all.

"You'll see," he said.

She did her best to let go of her disappointment. "Sure," she said. "I can take it slow."

Another kiss. He'd call her. It wasn't the end of the evening she'd expected or wanted. She watched him walk toward Seventh Avenue until he rounded the corner in the direction of the subway. It was late, the avenue bright with street and shop lights, people walked briskly in the cold. Kay's street was still. Most of the windows in the brownstones had gone dark. The trees looked as sullen as she did. Sitting on the top of the stoop, she wrapped her arms around her knees and sulked.

Later that night as she lay in bed, she felt a gentle nudge inside of her, and picked up the pen and journal.

Hollis T. Miller

A woman has a right to her desires—her desire for love, for sex, for a career, for adventure, for a family. She chooses. It's her life to discern, not for another to dictate to her. What is worth her while? What is a waste of her time? She chooses who comes with her. If they don't want to come, she keeps going. Her strength is going into the depths and reaching for the heights and never defining herself by someone else's desire for her—it is her desire for her life that strengthens her and brings her into being.

This voice felt bigger than her own, its strength startled and comforted her. She pulled the covers over her and with each breath imagined herself sinking to the bottom of the ocean, into the silky silt and infinite quiet where sleep finally took her under.

Eleven

The next day Charlene and Dido's usual romp and ruckus woke Kay early and she wasn't having it. It was a Sunday for God's sake. She took her fist and pounded the wall. "Give it up, Charlene!" she yelled, "I'm trying to sleep!" Charlene's high-pitched solo suddenly sounded like a deflating balloon. Silence. It didn't matter though. She couldn't fall back asleep. The bedroom was chilled. The morning light through her window, gray.

The clothes she'd so meticulously picked out for her date with Peter the night before were in a heap on the floor. On her nightstand near the window, the plant she'd bought just after her breakup with Rodin had dried into crusty, brown tentacles. It looked like a dead sea creature. Her mind was groggy and agitated. A familiar loneliness woke up in her chest. It was as if she'd lost something but couldn't recall what she'd lost. She tried to push the feeling away, but it just came right back. It couldn't have been because Peter didn't stay the night. That seemed a shallow reason for this heaviness that pressed down on her. *Get out of bed and get going.* Maybe she could outrun the feeling, escape its descent. She took the bin of winter clothes out from under her bed and bundled herself in a wool sweater, scarf, hat, and her down coat. Then she dug out her winter boots from inside the closet. A touch of moisturizer on her skin, a bit of lip gloss to the lips, and a coat of mascara to her eyelashes, she looked fresher, but felt worn out.

At the bodega on the corner, she bought a cup of coffee with milk then walked toward Prospect Park. The trees looked cold with their crooked, naked branches; the row houses warm and opulent—stained glass windows and early-nineteenth-century masonry. Her favorite thing to do on the weekends was to walk to Prospect Park and imagine what it would be like to be one of the families who lived in these homes. In her mind they were happy families: The parents loved each other and their children. On Saturday mornings the kids would slide down the long mahogany banister into the living room and race into the kitchen around the marble island where their father made pancakes and their mother squeezed fresh orange juice. They'd play music, something upbeat like the Jackson 5; they would laugh, dance, and eat. It was a simple joy, a security and love that to Kay seemed nearly impossible to attain. At least she could imagine it.

Her second favorite thing to do was to watch the dogs in Prospect Park run amok. Everyone in Park Slope who owned a dog must have been sent a memo from the Secret Dog Society that this was the place to be. Thirty dogs or more gathered with their owners on the grass each morning before 7:00 a.m. and this morning was no exception. The owners let their dogs off their leashes to run free and wild. Indifferent to the cold, they sniffed each other's rear ends, competed for thrown balls and Frisbees. In utter bliss they raced and nipped at each other's heels with smiles on their rough, furry faces. It softened her to watch them, to see that even dogs could live happily in the City.

The Heart Line

She sat on a bench and watched a basset hound nearly trip over its ears as it loped after a border collie. A gray and black dappled Australian shepherd ran up to Kay and dropped a ball in front of her. The dog's tongue hung limp from its panting mouth as it pranced back and forth from its hind to front legs looking from Kay to a lanky man in a gray beanie, heavy green jacket, and jeans who walked toward them in long, steady strides.

"Lucky, come." He had an English accent. The dog quickly picked up the ball and brought it to him. The man lobbed it over a tree and then, instead of following the dog, continued to walk toward Kay.

"I was hoping to see you again," he said as he approached. She looked him over carefully—about her same age, if not a little older, with dark blue eyes that radiated an intensity she tried not to squirm under.

"Again?" She had no idea who he was.

"You had turkey dinner at my place the other night." He gave her a cheeky smile.

She was lost. "Your place?"

"Well, it's not exactly *my* place."

She studied him, the long, straight nose. "Ohhh. You're the waiter who sent me that note."

He rolled his hand and bowed. "It is I."

"Are you an actor?"

"How could you tell?"

She smiled at his eagerness. "You wait tables and have a certain flare for the dramatic . . . I don't remember you having an accent though."

"That's strange, isn't it? It's what most American women remember about me . . . May I?" he asked, gesturing toward the bench.

"Certainly," she said, and he sat down next to her. Lucky had run up again with the ball and dropped it. He threw it again.

"Bruno," he said turning toward her and extending his gloved hand.

She shook it. "Bruno?"

"I know, everyone says I don't look like a Bruno. I should grow a beard or dye my hair black."

She hadn't thought any such thing, only that Bruno was an uncommon name. "I'm Kay."

"I don't know any Kays," he said. "That's a lovely name." His teeth began to chatter. He slapped his hands to his thighs and rubbed them furiously. "It's bloody cold, isn't it? Forgot to put on my long underwear. Damn dog will chew up everything in the flat if I don't take him out for at least an hour to run, which is brutal this time of year."

"It is. I can hardly feel my face."

"It's serendipitous running into you like this. Don't you think?"

She shrugged. She hadn't known who he was, so it wasn't serendipitous to her.

He was looking back and forth between Kay and the dog, which was exchanging sniffs with a terrier. "I'd like to take you out."

He sure got down to it. "Um. Maybe."

"Maybe she says. You play hard to get."

"Actually, I'm horrible at games. And considering this is the first time we've ever really spoken I'd hardly say I was playing hard to get."

"Can I have your number?"

He didn't let up. "Why don't you give me yours?"

"I'll never hear from you if I leave it up to you. I know it."

"You don't know that." She felt like they were two children playing on a playground. It was rather enjoyable.

"I can feel it."

"You'll just have to wait and see."

"I hate that. It's like going on an audition. Do you know how often I have to wait and see? Most of the time I just wait, wait, wait. I never see . . ." (She started laughing. Who was this guy?) "Well, at least I can make you laugh. That's something." She couldn't help but laugh. He was simultaneously confident and insecure, annoying and charming. He was a pleading child, a live wire. "I really thought my accent and debonair style would win you over."

"It takes a little more than that."

"You're a serious-minded woman—I could tell that in the restaurant. OK. I'll give you my number just as long as you promise to call me once, even it's just to say, 'Sorry, Bruno, it's not going to happen' and that can be in a week or six months. I just want to hear from you."

"You won't remember me in six months." Lucky came up again with the ball and this time she threw it.

"You underestimate yourself, Kay. By the way, your nose is bright pink. A little rose."

She squeezed it between her fingers. "I can't feel it."

"Your lips are blue too. How about a cup of tea? It's the perfect remedy."

Bruno tied Lucky to a bike rack outside the Cocoa Bar.

"Isn't he going to freeze?" asked Kay.

"He's a dog with a good coat of fur. He's meant to brave the elements. He'll be fine."

The warm aroma of coffee enveloped them. Bruno insisted she let him order and prepare the tea. They spent the morning playing chess and sipping English breakfast, which she noted was quite delicious with the hefty dose of sugar and milk. He was a better chess player, and she made a pact with herself to practice. It seemed a worthwhile endeavor.

Bruno gave her exactly what she needed that morning: attention. Nothing could substitute for the feeling of being seen and wanted by someone else. Peter had completely confused her the night before, she didn't know how to read him, but Bruno was practically transparent. It was refreshing. She still wouldn't give him her number but took his.

"Maybe," she said again as they stood on the street corner saying good-bye. Lucky jumped up and down doing pirouettes in the air.

"I'm gutted," he said. "A whole morning with me and you still don't know I'm fantastic."

"I know you're fantastic. That has nothing to do with it."

"Why not? It should." He peered at her.

"I have . . . stuff."

"Ah, stuff. Mysterious stuff . . . You have a boyfriend?"

She hesitated. "No. Just stuff."

"Uh-huh. All right. Well, know this," he put his hand over his heart, "I'll wait for you, Kay."

She laughed and kissed him on the cheek. Despite his ability to uplift her spirits, she couldn't take him seriously. He expressed himself too easily. She imagined he was this forward with any woman he found even mildly attractive. It was important to remember he was an actor.

On her walk home she couldn't stop smiling until she thought about Bruno's question: *You have a boyfriend?* She stopped and a chill traveled through her.

Peter had a girlfriend, of course he did. Why these starts and stops? The urgency and hesitation? He didn't know how to handle his situation. A girlfriend. She just knew it. And the heavy feeling of rejection and disappointment that had seized her, now compressed into a dense tightness and caught fire. He lied to her. Gazed into her eyes and constructed a fantasy, making plans with her when he had no business making plans with anyone. She wanted to hit something.

In her apartment she paced. The guttural sound of an animal came from her. Her hands shook. She took the Ajax from under her kitchen sink and scattered it all over her bathroom. She attacked every piece of tile and grout with a scouring brush and religious ferocity. She diluted bleach in water and mopped the five-square feet of the bathroom floor. She started on the kitchen, emptying out the refrigerator, wiping out food residue, washing the stovetop and counters, and finally threw out every pickled piece of food. She swept the wood floors, dusted shelves, and rearranged the clothes in her drawers and closet. Three hours later she lay on her bed exhausted. Fool, she told herself. Fool!

Her phone pinged. She rolled over and reached for it on her nightstand. Peter had texted: *I had a great time last night. Looking forward to next time.* She lifted her finger to respond, but what could she say? Instead, she put the phone down and picked up her journal and pen from her dresser.

You don't have to please. You don't need approval. Be true.

Twelve

Carlos and Nikki were huddled around Amita's cubicle when Kay approached from the break room with a cup of coffee. Carlos gripped the cubicle wall, threw his head back as if he was riding a rollercoaster and cackled.

"Shhh," said Nikki. "You always forget where you are."

"How is everyone this morning?" asked Kay.

"Kay-Kay! You won't believe it," said Carlos.

"He's got a man," said Nikki, and Carlos slapped her shoulder.

"Woman, why you always gotta go and steal my thunder."

Amita, with a playful grin, typed and sang under her breath, "You gotta man? I gotta a man . . ."

Stephen Colby, a partner who was more than six feet tall and looked like he should be gracing the cover of *GQ* magazine rather than the halls of Preeny walked by and a hush passed through the whole group. "Good morning, everyone." He gave the group a wink and a nod. He walked with breezy confidence like he had the world on a string.

Once he was out of sight Nikki snapped her fingers. "He's the one partner who could ask me to lie down and I'd be on my back in two seconds."

The Heart Line

"He'd never ask," said Carlos.

"Shut up," said Nikki and she punched his shoulder.

"Carlos, who's this man?" Kay asked.

"His name is Tony. He's from Cameroon. And he is hot and all mine, all mine."

"He's your boyfriend?" asked Kay.

"He's something," said Carlos. Then Carlos's eyes focused on something behind Kay. "Amita," he said, "one of your crew is about to arrive. We're outta here. Let's catch up later." Nikki and Carlos left, and when Kay turned around Peter stood in front of her.

"Why good morning, Ms. Manning." His tone was so bright and welcoming, for a second, she didn't want to disappoint him. She gave him a reluctant smile. He twitched but kept up the tight professional persona. "How are you?"

"I'm fine. You're working from the office this week?" she inquired.

"Now I am. We had a meeting with the client this morning and they said we're making the employees nervous. They asked us to work off-site the next couple of weeks. Do you have a minute after I speak with Amita?" he said.

"Amita's your assistant?"

Amita kept focused on her computer while she nodded along with Peter.

"She is and I consider myself very lucky, although I don't think she feels the same. There are five of us that rely on her." Amita continued to nod. He handed her a Post-it. "These are the four partners I need to get in the same conference room at the same time with the client. It needs to happen before Thanksgiving. I'm sorry, I don't envy your task."

It was nearly an impossible task. The partners were notorious for canceling big meetings last minute so they could attend other bigger meetings. Loyalties shifted depending on how big the client was and how senior the Preeny partner. It could take a few weeks or longer to schedule a big meeting, and if one of the partners canceled the assistant would have to start over. It wasn't just about securing a meeting time either, food had to be ordered, a conference room had to be booked. And everyone wanted a conference room with a view and if a view wasn't available, well, the partners rarely withheld expressing their dissatisfaction to the assistant—the assistant who spent the entire day scheduling multiple meetings, more than half of which would need to be rescheduled at least two or three times. It was just one act of futility after another, and in Amita's case, escaping this existence was all the incentive she needed to pursue her education and carve out a niche for herself. Kay secretly rooted for her.

"It would be nice to be envied," said Amita. Her eyes forlorn, she took the Post-it, and then, before she succumbed to the pull of her computer, her head popped up. "Sarah called. She said she'd meet you in front of Lincoln Center at six forty-five."

Kay felt like she'd just been pinched as she watched him take a shallow breath and respond with a quiet, "Thanks."

"Your girlfriend. Your girlfriend, Sarah. Right?" said Kay. Focused on getting to the truth, she didn't care that Amita's eyes had suddenly grown two sizes, shocked by the realization that she'd unwittingly revealed a secret and as a result discovered there was something going on between Peter and Kay.

Peter passed a hand over his mouth as if to draw words out of it. "Can we take that minute in your office now?" he said.

She did her best to remain mindful of her professional composure; the walls of her office were glass and anyone who passed by would be alerted to something heated between them if she couldn't cool the fire that was rising from her feet to her head. The way his shoulders and head slumped toward the ground made him seem so guilty. His defense was weak and typical: he was trying to get himself out of a complicated situation; he hadn't been thinking clearly; he didn't want to hurt his girlfriend and he didn't want to hurt her.

She stood with all the energy and erectness of a righteous person. "You should have just told me the truth. I might have waited for you to figure out your situation." His eyes wide and helpless, she clenched her jaw to try to maintain control. "You know what all the support staff call the consultants?" she asked. He shook his head. "Risk averse, insecure overachievers." The anger was hot and bitter inside of her, she had to spit it out. She only got angrier when she thought of how she'd told him about her family situation. The only other person who knew about it was Maddy. He had to have the denseness of a bull to avoid telling her the truth when she'd suffered a betrayal so deep.

"I didn't sleep with you," he said. "I wanted to, but I didn't."

She let that comment sit in the air for a moment.

"Congratulations. You're free and clear of any wrongdoing." She gathered her laptop, shoved it into her purse then lifted her coat off the hook behind her before she pushed past him and through the door.

In the lobby she texted her supervisor: *Jane, I'm feeling sick. Heading home and will work from there.*

The subway was too dark and claustrophobic. She needed to walk. Down Park Avenue through the MetLife Building, down the escalators, and into the cavern of Grand Central Station, where the gods in their constellations above her watched quietly the dizzying speed of the city in transit. Quickly and purposefully, she walked, like she knew where she was going, except she had no idea. An hour later she found herself in Chinatown: cobbled streets, bright red signs with gold script,

Peking ducks hung from a wire inside a shop window, featherless and burnt-looking. Trash bags lined the sidewalks, which otherwise were fairly empty. The only benefits of the cold were fewer people on the street and the absence of the city stench that was part of the landscape in the warmer months. The sky was whitewashed, it was too frigid. As long as she kept walking, she couldn't feel it. A skin of sweat formed underneath her clothes. On Canal Street she passed a monstrous peach building with a sign advertising massage and acupuncture. Panting, she crossed the West Side Highway into Hudson River Park. She walked to the end of one of the piers and listened to the hollow plunk of her shoes against the wood planks while the water sloshed beneath and around her. At the pier's edge, the wind slapped her like a cold, angry hand.

She felt fragile, embarrassed. She'd wanted to fall in love, to be seen and held by love. For a moment, he made her feel this, but it wasn't true. So now what?

Now nothing, she thought.

She wondered if there had been even a sliver of something real between them. Across the river she took in Jersey, the low redbrick buildings and newer modern ones with their sleek metal frames. It was underwhelming compared to New York. She leaned into the railing and watched a run-down tugboat make its way upriver. The sweat on her skin cooled to a frost and her teeth chattered. When her anger expired, she caught the subway at Canal Street back to Brooklyn.

Thirteen

Had he actually thought he was going to pull off a seamless transition from one life into another? No. It was absurd to think he would be able to bypass explaining his relationship with Sarah to Kay. He hadn't meant to do it, but there was no way Kay was going to accept that as an excuse. He hadn't thought it through. He'd been feeling and fantasizing, not thinking. The fantasies love conjures up don't coexist with common sense.

Of course Sarah was going to leave a text message, a voice mail, and when he didn't respond to either within thirty minutes, a message with Amita to let him know what time to meet. And of course Kay would be there at the exact time Amita relayed the message.

Of course.

Sarah bought season tickets to the opera last spring and usually went with a girlfriend but had made him promise to go with her to the *Marriage of Figaro* performance, which was tonight, and he wasn't allowed to use work as an excuse to get out of it. He didn't much care for opera, he thought of it as something his grandparents might attend. The over-the-top expression wasn't something he could relate to, but Sarah loved it—the singing, the costumes, the sets, the whole spectacle. He told the team he'd be back after the performance. And he told himself to just go through the motions, get through the evening, and he'd think of what to do about Kay later. He needed time.

The light through the Met's arches glowed gold. He expected to find Sarah inside within its warmth, so that when he noticed the woman with the ankle-length camel hair coat sitting next to the outside fountain, a light mist rising behind her, he had to look twice before he recognized her. She had combed her hair out long and straight, wore bright lipstick, and dark eyeliner, which made her eyes pop like two blue beacons. She looked sleek, sophisticated. He walked briskly toward her, expecting her to stand up and walk toward him, but she remained seated.

He leaned down to kiss her. "Are you ready?" He asked.

"Not yet." She patted her hand on the concrete bench. He looked at his watch and raised his shoulders to his ears.

"It's freezing."

"This won't take long."

This. Oh no, he thought and then sat next to her. "You look very pretty," he said.

"Thank you." The smile across her lips made him think she had a secret.

"What is it?" he asked.

He watched her reach into her coat pocket, take out a baby blue box, and place it between them.

"You tell me," she said. Her smile bordered the edge of glee.

He stared at the box, unable to move. His heart sprinted into his throat and he coughed; he couldn't swallow it back down. After a moment he picked up the box and opened it. There was the ring he'd bought, glittering at him. He'd nearly forgotten about it.

"Sarah—"

The Heart Line

"Peter," she grabbed his hand and squeezed it, "I thought you could use some help."

He couldn't tell if he was shaking from shock or cold. "When did you find it?"

"About three weeks ago. I know you've been waiting for the perfect moment, but there isn't one. I feel like an idiot for doubting you. I'm so sorry." He could see waves crashing within her. "I've been holding this excitement forever and I just couldn't go on pretending like I didn't know."

The pressure rested on him, nearly impossible to dislodge. The emotion in her face, the hope, the dream coming true was unbearable to witness. Simultaneously, he wrestled with the revelation that she'd found the ring. She'd gone through his things? Had she intentionally snooped in hopes of finding a ring? You don't accidentally stumble upon a Tiffany box *in the back* of someone's nightstand drawer unless you're looking for something. The usual nagging questions surfaced: Did she want to marry him? Or did she just want to marry? He sucked in the freezing air to catch his breath. He didn't know how to ask her these questions. Maybe these were questions he should have asked himself because here he was at the pivotal moment of the rest of his life, and he still didn't know what to do. She'd forced it upon him: The chance to shut the door on all of his confusion and move forward once and for all. Make a decision. Here was the ring. There was the girl he had meant it for. Now ask the question.

It wasn't even a Tiffany ring. It was a lie. A hot shame pounded inside of him. He didn't know how to be truthful with the woman he'd spent more than five years of his life with. He'd wanted to please her. He'd always been happy to coast along in her wake, comforted by the security of her certainty. She had the right education, the right family, the right ambitions, the right look. It was a life he could walk into without thinking and he thought it would give him immunity to the unexpected forces that terrified him—the force that took his dad, but also the force that brought him Kay and was beating at the door inside of him.

He'd lost Kay, but even without her, he couldn't do this now. There it was plain and clear: he didn't love her.

"Sarah, I am . . . I-I'm so sorry."

At first, she broke a smile like he'd told an incredible joke. Then she seemed to piece together the words and their meaning, and her face fell. Her head shook with confusion. He watched her anger rise then crumble and thought she might hit him. Her eyes lay on him, but she wasn't looking at him. She'd gone somewhere else, squinted at him and leaned her head in like she might ask a question. Her bottom lip quivered. The blow stunned her. He felt it too—the expectations, the plans, the history, the future, their time together unraveling.

A sudden breath and she was back from wherever she'd gone. "I'm sorry too," she said. For a split second grief broke on her face, but she quickly composed herself.

He wanted to console her, "Sarah—"

"No," she said. "No."

Her hands pressed against her coat. She stood up. "I'm going to watch Figaro." Her voice unsteady yet determined. "When I get home, I don't want you to be there." As he watched her walk toward the bright lights of the Met, the chandeliers sparkling through the long windows, he almost called out to her to come back. To have watched Kay's anger and disappointment, and then to see Sarah walk away without any resistance made him feel like the loneliest man in the world.

He grabbed the blue box, leaned his face over the fountain pool and heaved. Was he hot or cold? It felt like forever before he was able to stand up and walk away.

The Heart Line

He forced himself back to the moment, to his feet on the sidewalk, the sleet falling, the rushing and honking of cars all around him. The plan the past three years had been to marry Sarah and now there was no plan. He walked toward the subway, drawing the arm of his sleeve back to look at his watch. She'd return from the opera in three hours. He'd respect her wishes and get out even though they needed to talk. He owed her an explanation. There had to be something more to say after so many years together.

His friends were few and far between in the City and most of them were his and Sarah's friends. He called Troy Berger, a smart, eager-to-please associate on his team. The other junior members on his team were women and therefore completely out of the question to call for a favor.

At the subway entrance he wiped away a ring of slush that had collected around his collar while he waited for Troy to pick up. "Peter?"

"Troy," said Peter, "I need a place to stay for a couple of nights." Troy hesitated then explained he had two other roommates. They were clean, frugal young men, which made living in cramped quarters just bearable, that and the fact that they only really used the apartment to sleep. Another body in that space seemed impossible though. Peter listened while Troy worked out the problem, ("We do have a couch . . ."). Quiet attention was all the influence he had to exert for Troy to graciously offer it up and explain to his roommates that he couldn't say no to the team manager.

Done. Next. Peter walked down into the roar of the tunnel.

Benny, the doorman, was the gatekeeper of the basement and nervously fingered the elevator key to that floor around his neck like it was the coveted ring from *The Hobbit*. He kept one foot inside the elevator and the other in the hallway while Peter wrestled two suitcases from the coffin-sized storage unit he and Sarah paid extra for. "You goin' on a nice trip, Mr. Bowen?"

"Something like that."

It was a natural question, but Benny should have known not to ask questions, particularly about one's comings and goings, particularly because this was New York, and he was the doorman and had keys. Peter liked Benny though, he was always friendly and his six-foot, four-inch frame with a chest and arms like the Rock of Gibraltar made Peter feel like he had a personal bodyguard looking out for him. He was going to miss having a doorman. There was the added security and convenience, but also, he had to admit, he liked the status symbol.

Once he made it into the apartment, Peter managed to pack most of his clothes and all his toiletries in the two suitcases. Beyond that it wasn't clear what really belonged to him and what really belonged to her. He scanned their small living area. He had paid for the couch, so technically it was his. Only considering she picked it out and spent so much time persuading him to buy it, he felt like it was hers, and she likely did too. There was the coffee table, the end tables, and the handsome barrister bookcases against the far wall, which they found at an estate sale when they spent a fall weekend in Vermont.

He gave himself two options: (1) let her have all the stuff in the apartment: all the furniture, bedding, kitchenware, anything they collected or bought while they were together, it was the least he could do for failing her, a kind of settlement; (2) he'd take the couch, or she could buy it from him, and he'd take a set of sheets, some plates and silverware. She could have everything else. Either way it seemed right that she would get most of the stuff.

The Heart Line

He didn't have to decide tonight, they'd talk, count and divide spoons and plates together or whatever people do after a breakup. And he'd forgotten about the bed they'd bought when they moved in. It was a grown-up bed with a grown-up price, and grown-up comfort. He might negotiate for that bed . . . if he could shelve the guilt that descended upon him when he thought about how she wouldn't be able to afford the apartment on her own. He wondered if she'd ask her parents for help, probably not, she had a healthy level of pride and wouldn't want to set up that kind of dependency, even if they offered it.

It was too risky to think about all the inconveniences his leaving would create for her. It interfered with the wave of energy propelling him forward and he wasn't going to try to stop it anymore. Sometimes things just don't work out, and who is to say who the guilty party is? In Sarah's mind there was no doubt he was the one to blame. But can you blame a person for falling out of love with you? Can you blame a person for not knowing if they were ever in love with you? He gripped the handle of the suitcase on either side of him, opened the door, and walked out.

Fourteen

The cigarette tasted stale. Kay wasn't any good at smoking, yet she enjoyed the slightly sweet taste of tobacco on her lips, and it gave her something to do when she was listless. She kept a pack stashed in a kitchen drawer for times when she felt distressed or sad. The past few days at work she hadn't seen Peter. He was camping out in a conference room with his team, working on a slide deck for the client, so he might as well have been on the moon. Teams rarely came up for air in the week before a major presentation. She expected more from him though. She expected him to provide more of an explanation for his behavior, to at least try to save face in hopes of repairing the delicate connection between them. Maybe she expected too much. Unable to come to any kind of resolution on her own, she went out on her fire escape to smoke a cigarette.

The bright yellow of the sun changed to a warm, rich orange that turned the edge of the clouds pink as it descended below the row of houses behind her building. She blew small puffs of smoke into the air and peered down into the backyard of the house behind her apartment. A rope swing hung from a thick tree branch.

The Heart Line

The backyards in Brooklyn or any part of the city lacked the size of those she had grown up with in California, but to have even a patch of grass or a garden here was a privilege and a kind of precious secret amid all the concrete, mortar, and brick. This was a stately brick row house that had been updated with long modern windows and, in addition to its yard, crowned with a roof garden, which was lush in the summer, but in the last six weeks had shed its leaves. There was a small greenhouse at the center of the roof that sweated from the inside and she wondered what kind of botanical treasures grew within it.

Through the basement windows of the house, she could see a young girl, maybe seven or eight, sitting at the kitchen table. A backpack open on the floor, the girl swung her legs back and forth while she dutifully did her homework. A woman, whom Kay assumed was the mother, sat beside her and watched over her daughter's progress with steady love.

She took another drag from her cigarette and shifted her gaze back to the sunset. Maybe her expectations of Peter were too high, or maybe they weren't high enough. These were the times when she wished she had a closer relationship with her mother because she could use some loving and sound counsel. Her family had pieced itself back together slowly over the years into a different structure. She credited her dad for being a forgiving person and not severing his relationship with her mom. They found a way to be civil with each other and that thread of decency between them was the only thing that kept Kay intact through an inconsolable time. She still struggled to forgive her mom though. Her affair had been like a bomb in their home; she lit it and watched the pieces fall and burn. Physical and emotional distance seemed the only way to have some semblance of a healthy relationship with her. Otherwise, the waters between them became a swamp, a quicksand she couldn't find her way out of.

What terrified her the most was that her mother was in her blood, her being, and as much as she wanted to believe she could be her own person, she swore she could hear her mother's voice coming through her own sometimes. She wondered if her own deep need to find a love was the same as her mom's need, a need so desperate she sought to satiate it at whatever cost.

Maybe true love was a myth. It perpetuated all kinds of expectations and dreams, which any human being would inevitably fail to live up to. She had made Peter into some kind of hero or prince. He was going to whisk her off to Mendocino. They were going to laugh, make memories, and share an intimacy so deep it would take away the loneliness that had followed her around like a shadow most of her life.

After she'd confronted Peter that day in her office and walked to the pier and stared at the river and become so cold she thought her bones might snap, she finally made it home, where she prepared herself a hot, bitter cup of coffee, and thought about what to do. Later, she scrolled through her phone's contacts and made a call. Then she walked to Seventh Street between Eighth Avenue and Prospect Park West where she stopped in front of a red and sand-colored limestone home. Ornate cement molding framed the door and a beautiful stained-glass window sat above a larger picture window, through which she could see a chandelier inside, its bulbs shone like small suns. Cement stairs zigged up one way and zagged another like a maze from the sidewalk to the front door—a burnished chestnut frame and body of wrought iron and glass. On the other side of it a long banister descended from the upper floors and coiled like a snake at its end.

The Heart Line

She looked for multiple mailboxes and buzzers to indicate that the home was actually apartments. When she didn't find any, she thought she may have taken down the wrong address. A dog barked as soon as she rang the doorbell. "Down boy!" She heard from the other side of the door. When Bruno opened it Lucky excitedly plunged his nose into Kay's groin and licked furiously at her hand as she gently pushed the dog away.

"Behave, Lucky. You're embarrassing me." Bruno pulled the dog by the collar back into the house. His feet were bare, and he wore loose-fitted jeans and a long sleeve navy cotton shirt. From under his disheveled hair, he gave Kay a playful smile. "Kay, it's wonderful to see you again." He extended his arm wide and bowed as if he were a midcentury butler welcoming a guest. "Please, come in."

"Thank you."

He took her coat and hung it on a coat stand in the foyer then led her into the living room where there was a fire burning in the fireplace.

"Now I debated about turning the fire off because I thought you'd think it such an obvious seduction move—truth is I had that fire going long before you called. It gets bloody cold in here despite having the heat on full blast."

"I like the fire."

"Fantastic." He clapped and rubbed his hands together. "Who wants to take off their clothes first?" Before her mouth dropped completely, he backpedaled. "That was in poor taste. Breaking the ice requires a bit of awkwardness and I'm just so good at being awkward. Forgive me?"

"Forgiven," she said. Bruno was too comical for her to feel threatened by him.

"Thank you." Then he directed his hands toward the back of the house. "I thought some hot tea and biscuits would be nice—

or if you'd prefer hot chocolate or coffee I can accommodate. An Englishman, however, must always have tea. I have it set up in the kitchen. I would have made a roast, but I need a bit more notice for that." He was visibly nervous, running his hands through his hair, looking at her intently to gauge her response to him.

In the kitchen was a large butcher block island where he'd arranged an assortment of cookies on a plate. Behind the butcher block he lit the stove, an artifact from another era with four long legs and a worn yellow and green enamel finish. He placed a black kettle on the flame. He sat on one side of the island and she on the other; Lucky sat beside her with his face pointed toward her, hopeful for her attention or some food. Bruno leaned in and looked at Kay with such an intense gaze she had to consciously resist looking away.

"You have no idea how surprised I was that you called."

"I surprised myself," she said.

He studied her. "That 'stuff' you spoke of—what happened to it?"

She pressed her lips together, opened her mouth to speak and then didn't know what to say.

"I know," he continued, "I just get right down to it, don't I?"

"You really do."

He tapped his knuckles on the island twice and shortly afterward the kettle whistled.

"Do you want something besides tea? I mean I thought about wine. Would you prefer that? I just don't know what exactly is appropriate. I want to be here for you. For whatever stuff you're going through."

"You're sweet."

"*Sweet!* It's the kiss of death."

"It is not."

The Heart Line

"So you just want tea?"

She nodded.

He went about making the tea silently. Kay found his presence comforting. The kitchen was full and warm; he moved about it with a familiar ease. Lucky transitioned from sitting to lying on the floor, the dog's eyes drawn upward, they shifted back and forth between the two humans, intent on their every sound and movement.

Bruno set a mug in front of her, added a teaspoon of sugar, and from a flowered porcelain pot poured black tea into it, followed by a dollop of milk.

She took in the space. "Do you live alone?"

"I do right now. Occasionally I let a room to some of my actor friends when they're in a tough spot. I'm a dream landlord. I rarely collect rent and of course it makes it nearly impossible to get rid of them. Yet I do get rid of them because, to be honest, I prefer to live alone."

"Really? One floor isn't enough for you? You need the whole house?"

"It's like this: Actors, if they're serious, practice. And you need space to practice—to be Hamlet, Hannibal, Richard the Third, or whomever. Although some of an actor's work is research and study, the other part is physical and loud and messy. I'm not comfortable with people witnessing that process."

The home must have had four floors. "You're a working actor? You book gigs?"

Bruno let out a subtle laugh. "Ah, yes—what you mean to ask is how do I afford this grand home?"

"Sorry, I didn't mean to be tactless."

"Not at all. I'd be curious too . . . Like most actors, I work occasionally, that is, I occasionally get paid. The house belongs to my parents—my mother. It's an heirloom really. My mother grew up in it and then went to college in England where she met my father. We visited my grandparents a lot when I was growing up and they left my mum the house, which she has graciously put in my care for as long as I desire."

"It's a beautiful home."

"It's not bad," he said and looked up like he was assessing the craftsmanship of the tiled ceiling and wood beams that stretched the length of the kitchen.

They made small talk for a while: the cold, holiday plans, her work, his morning exercise routine, and the role he'd recently played off-Broadway in *Antony and Cleopatra*.

Then he wanted to know how she filled her soul. Those were his words: *fill your soul*. Her soul seemed to growl from hunger at the mention of its name. How long had she neglected it? She used to read poetry, go to poetry readings and open mics, watch obscure films in small independent film houses, memorize the lyrics to musicals, spend an entire evening with her nose buried in a novel, but since moving to New York she'd become preoccupied with survival, working a job that didn't reach any part of her soul, and which left her little time for much else. "It's ironic, isn't it?" he noted, "To lose touch with that part of yourself when you're in one of the cultural epicenters of the world? It happens all the time. The City demands too much from us. Life demands so much. It's constant work to keep in contact with our soul. I know how lucky I am to have this house. It eases the pressure."

She nibbled on a cookie. He spoke a language that was foreign and familiar. "Yes," she said. "I feel like I'm caught in a structure that was created by someone else, and it doesn't fit me. I just don't remember how to function any other way."

The Heart Line

"I think you start by asking the question: How can I live differently? How do I really want to live? Each day you try to answer that question. You try to do something that answers it."

She considered she had underestimated him. Because here, underneath his quick rhythm and wit, was a more measured, thoughtful man.

"Acting feeds your soul?"

"Most of the time it does. Actors seek the truth, which I find quite noble. I've always wanted to be part of their tribe."

"Will you recite some of your lines from *Anthony and Cleopatra*?"

He ticked his tongue against the roof of his mouth and shook his head. "You know exactly how to get to an actor's heart. But I don't know, you seem awfully hard to impress."

"Please. I'll give you lots of praise."

"And if you don't like it?"

"I'll give you lots of praise."

"Ha!"

She batted her eyelashes at him. He couldn't resist.

"I won't torture you with the entire thing," he said. Seated on the stool, he closed his eyes for a moment, cleared his throat, and shifted his position. When he opened his eyes again, he looked right at her. "This is Enobarus from Antony and Cleopatra." He leaned forward with a wicked grin.

> I will tell you.
> The barge she sat in, like a burnish'd throne,
> Burn'd on the water: the poop was beaten gold;
> Purple the sails, and so perfumed, that
> The winds were love-sick with them, the oars were silver,
> Which to the tune of flutes kept stroke, and made

> The water which they beat to follow faster,
> As amorous of their strokes. For her own person,
> It beggar'd all description; she did lie
> In her pavilion,—cloth-of-gold of tissue,—
> O'er-picturing that Venus where we see
> The fancy outwork nature; on each side her
> Stood pretty dimpled boys, like smiling Cupids,
> With divers-colour'd fans, whose wind did seem
> To glow the delicate cheeks which they did cool,
> And what they undid did.

The tenor of his voice reverberated in the room. The image of gold and purple, the glistening water the oars beat against, and Cleopatra lounging in her beauty and regality fanned by the adoration of all, lingered in her mind.

"That was sexy," she said.

"Really?" He looked pleased with himself.

"Sexier than tea and biscuits."

"Come on, now. Are you making fun of my biscuits?" She stood up and walked to his side of the island. He turned to face her and when she was so close there was less than an inch between them, he wrapped his arms around her waist.

"I like your biscuits just fine," she said and kissed him.

Kay coughed out the final drag from her cigarette and snuffed it against the fire escape. She shivered thinking of her encounter with Bruno. The sunset still illuminated the sky, and she wouldn't go in until it turned dark.

Calling Bruno had been a calculated move; she couldn't bear being alone with her disillusionment. The situation with Peter was still present. She didn't let go of things easily, but after barely two dates how could she hold on? How easily she got carried away.

She looked again through the window of the house where the girl and the mother sat at the table. It grew dark as she watched the young girl put away her homework and begin to set the table for dinner. The mother moved to the stove and stirred something in a pot. Kay yearned for such communal and fundamental rituals and hoped that one day she'd be able to create as much in her own life.

Fifteen

Sarah slept soundly the night she returned home from the Met; it was the following two nights that were intolerable. When the apartment was as quiet as any apartment in New York can be, she became aware of the absence of his body next to hers. Often, when Peter was there, she woke up in the middle of the night afraid, pursued by something but unsure of what or who it was, and as soon as she extended her arm across him, she would fill with calm and fall back asleep. Tonight, she grabbed his pillow and inhaled his scent, sharp and sweet. Would she never be able to put her arm across him like that again?

He would call. He wouldn't be able to just walk away. It was a question of when he would call. She sighed, the last bit of exasperation exiting her system, she'd probably hear from him within the week. She got out of bed to make a cup of Ovaltine—growing up, her mom wouldn't let her drink hot chocolate and would make her Ovaltine instead, now she preferred it.

On the couch in the dark she crossed her legs, the mug warmed the inside of her hands, and she gazed at the door. To the right of it, long lines of shadow from the window blinds cut through a framed art print: sunset, a man (in khaki slacks and a white shirt) and a woman (in a coral sundress) standing side by side on the deck of a ship. Their hands rested on the railing as they looked across the ocean at a city—a silhouette of black with bright white circles, balloons of light, floating around it. Their arms and hands just touched. They were together sailing toward some adventure or coming home. Her parents bought the print while traveling through Italy and had it framed back in the States as a housewarming gift for her and Peter when they moved into this apartment. She had been surprised they picked out something that actually appealed to her. It was the image of her future.

And now it wasn't.

She hadn't cried yet. She couldn't feel anything. He wasn't supposed to be the one to call things off. In all the years they'd been together she'd always thought she was the one in control.

From the beginning, when she'd met him for the first time at the Sigma Chi party, she set the tone. Everyone had spring fever, the booze flowed, and all the young women flaunted their limbs, finally exposed but still pale from the winter. A few girls had danced atop the dining room table, the chandelier above them quaking. Brothers leaned against the walls and watched. The music made everyone as drunk as the booze. It was so loud inside the house conversation was impossible; they all drank and danced more. Sarah filled her red Solo cup with whatever was in the keg and walked through the house with her friend and roommate, Jen, toward the back deck where there was another keg. It was cool outside. He was on the deck standing next to a skinny guy with long blond hair who looked like he belonged on the West Coast. He, however, was clean cut with a kind of classic masculinity, and although she liked that, what appealed to her most about him was that he wasn't having any fun. He observed everything like he was on high alert, a spy, or a narc (and not a very good one). Then he noticed her or maybe it was her legs in those incredibly short shorts, but she knew she had his attention when she walked over to him and handed him her beer because, strangely, he didn't have one.

"You clearly need this more than I do," she said. He looked at the cup suspiciously. "I swear it won't kill you. You'll probably feel great after you've had two or three." She wondered if he had any idea how uptight he was. When he still didn't smile or say a single word, she got an uneasy feeling. *He's definitely a cop*, she thought. When he finally took a healthy gulp of the beer and wiped the drips from the sides of his mouth, she was taken aback by the genuine smile that broke on his face.

"You're right. It's just what I needed."

"Are you a pledge?" she asked.

"No. My friend Shane is." He pointed to the skinny guy who now sat on a lounge chair with her roommate. "He says if I want any kind of social life this is the way to go."

"Do you want any kind of social life?"

"Not this kind."

"Too lowbrow for you?"

He looked confused. "It's just not my thing." He took another sip of beer. "Are you in a sorority?"

"Yes. Don't hold it against me."

"I'll do my best." He didn't fit in here, but he didn't seem to care. "I'm Peter."

"Sarah."

She liked the unassuming drive in him, the seriousness. At twenty, she had been unusually focused on the long-term, on where her life was going and who would be able to go with her. She was surprised to find out he was from California and his friend, Shane, who must have been drunk because he was braiding Jen's hair while she giggled, was from Delaware. *Amateurs*, she thought.

Playing coy was a waste of time. Even though she was slightly put off that Peter didn't ask her out before he left the party, she didn't let it deter her when she ran into him in the library a week later. He was asleep, his head on the table, with a microbiology textbook spread out before him.

She leaned over and whispered in his ear, "Boo."

He jolted up and she moved just in time to avoid his head smacking her face. He stared at her with a long face and slack mouth.

"I know you," he said, coming out of his stupor. "Ss-arah."

"That's right," she said. "That textbook must be riveting."

He was half asleep, trying to wake up.

"May I see it?"

He kept staring at her, then suddenly he was shaking his head and handing it to her. "Sure."

She already had a pen out. She flipped the book open and on the front inside cover wrote in large yet elegant script her name and number.

"I thought you could use some help," she said, handing it back to him. "I'll see you later." The wonder and admiration on his face made it clear that she'd hooked him. As she walked away, she heard him say, "Absolutely."

She felt certain about him. Only now, sitting in the apartment by herself in the dark, she couldn't deny that he hadn't felt the same way.

Sixteen

By the time the weekend arrived Kay still hadn't seen or heard from Peter and considered she'd probably only hear from him again when he needed to be staffed. That Friday she left work early and took the subway to Grand Army Plaza in Park Slope so she could stop at the co-op on Union Street. As she exited the subway, she looked toward Prospect Park. The late afternoon was clear and crisp. A fat piece of sky opened up above the park lit by the yellow and red jewel-colored leaves below it. It made her stop on the corner. Colors as alive as the sun and impossible to ignore, yet people brushed by her, seemingly impervious to this oasis that bloomed in the middle of the mad pace of life. The trees extended their offer of peace and quiet from the incessant thrum of traffic on Flatbush Avenue. For a moment, Kay relaxed.

At the co-op she hummed to herself. Free of her normal impulse to elbow through the narrow and overcrowded aisles, she took her time placing various items in her basket: hard cheese, shrimp, pasta, a handful of basil, and as many brightly colored vegetables as she could find.

She was annoyed, however, when she missed the bus on Seventh Avenue. It meant a very long walk in the cold with her

The Heart Line

grocery bags to Sixth Street and then up four flights of stairs. By the time she entered her apartment and dropped the bags on the table, she was cold, sweaty, and ready to lie down.

Rest would have to come later, she had committed to cooking dinner, to establishing a new rhythm, to nurturing herself and carving out a life one small act at a time. She sorted the groceries, put her phone on speaker and dialed Maddy before she took a zucchini from the colorful medley of vegetables and began to slice it lengthwise. She had avoided calling Maddy for the past week because Maddy was often quick to give advice and let Kay know what she thought about such and such situation. Her delivery usually lacked the nuance and understanding that Kay's fragile ego needed.

So, it was no surprise five minutes into the conversation, after Kay checked in on the baby's progress, and heard about the skills in Maddy's burgeoning family—Casey was constructing a crib from an old dresser, and Maddy's future mother-in-law was knitting booties and a cap for the baby—that Maddy's tone turned flustered after she inquired how Kay's date with Peter had gone and instead Kay casually mentioned Bruno, "Actually, there's this guy, Bruno."

"Bruno? Who's Bruno?"

"Like I said, he's a guy. A man." She filled a pot with water and put it on the stove to boil.

"Who is he?" She sounded so alarmed.

This is when the cost of having Maddy see her through every heartache she'd ever experienced became clear: Maddy took authority in Kay's life, like an overprotective sister. There wasn't even the possibility of her withholding anything from Maddy. It would be a betrayal.

"He's an actor. He waited on me at a restaurant and then I ran into him at the park . . . A new friend." It was specific and vague, and she hoped it would be enough.

"Uh-huh. You had sex with him."

"Whoa. You can't just jump to that conclusion."

"Oh, I can't? It's in your voice. I know you . . . So did you?"

Why couldn't Maddy just rejoice that she'd gotten laid? Why did she feel like a scolded child? "Yes, I did. And you shouldn't moralize my sex life."

"Oh please, I am doing no such thing. But I know you and you don't just jump into bed with people. You're the one romance movies work their magic on. You have to feel something; you have some fantasy about love or where something is going before you ever sleep with someone. What happened to Peter? I could hear the wedding bells ringing when you talked about him. I was expecting a full report on your date and then you up and tell me you've slept with Bruno, whom you've never mentioned until now."

"Uh, it's more like you extracted it from me," said Kay. "Besides, time moves faster in the city."

"Meaning?"

"Meaning that was last weekend and the world has changed since then . . . he has a girlfriend." She started on the onion.

"A serious girlfriend?" asked Maddy.

"Serious enough that he lied about having one."

"You asked him if he had a girlfriend?"

"I didn't have to ask."

There was a long pause. "What are you chopping?"

"I'm making pasta primavera."

"For one?"

"And your point is?"

The Heart Line

"Look, if you really like Peter then don't just write him off. You need to figure out what happened."

"He lied. That's what happened."

"Did you ask him about it? Did you talk?"

"He should have told me."

"Maybe he was trying to figure out how."

"Please stop playing devil's advocate. Whose friend are you anyway? You don't even know him. If I say he's an asshole, then you should believe me." Tears streamed down her face from the onion fumes. Maddy's attention was like the sun shining through a magnifying glass, Kay couldn't bear the heat, and this was a burn. This was her experience. It was her pain, her baggage, her heartache, her sex life, and she didn't want to share it. No one could make it better for her. She knew Bruno wasn't an answer, but that didn't mean she couldn't enjoy his company. And she knew it wasn't really Peter who had broken her heart, or Rodin.

"Well, you want to know what I think?"

"No," she dabbed her eyes with the kitchen towel, "but I'm sure you're going to tell me."

"I think you liked Peter so much you went and fucked Bruno to get him out of your mind. And, you know, that's just not wise."

"I hate you right now. I'm twenty-five years old, I'm not supposed to be wise for at least another twenty years." Kay walked to the kitchen sink and splashed water in her eyes. Yes, Maddy had taken way too much liberty in her counsel over the years with Kay and it had to stop. She went back to the stove and spoke into the phone on the counter, her arms raised toward the ceiling. "Stop trying to be my mother and just be my friend. Aren't you the person who told me to break out and free myself a few weeks ago?"

"Believe it or not this is me being your friend and I do think you need to break out, but it just sounds like you're not thinking clearly."

"This guy lies to me and somehow you twist it into a moral issue I'm having. Bruno and I are consenting adults. It was very nice to be with him, by the way." She took a pan from the cupboard, turned on a burner, then added butter and olive oil.

She could hear Maddy breathing. "Okay. I'm sorry, really," she said. "I just don't want you to get hurt or taken advantage of."

Kay almost laughed. "*Please*, it's way too late for that."

She was grateful to Maddy for the concern and love she could never find elsewhere, but it would never substitute for the love she'd always craved from her parents. Maybe that void would always be there. The difference was she saw it now, she could name it, and she knew she couldn't annihilate the emptiness no matter how hard she tried. She'd live with it because she had a life in front of her to live, and maybe by living the emptiness would grow smaller and smaller, and maybe one day it would disappear. Maybe.

For now, she was going to say good-bye, finish making dinner, set the table, open a bottle of wine, and wait for Bruno to arrive.

Seventeen

It was just after 5:00 a.m., Kay was wide awake and thankfully not because of any noise coming from Charlene's apartment. (In fact, she hadn't heard any orgasms for a week and wondered if Charlene and Dildo had split up.) Lying on her side, she looked toward the windowsill and, in the dark, she could just make out the willowy fronds of the fern she bought earlier in the week to re-energize her space. A feng shui book she recently purchased gave her all kinds of tips on how to create opportunities instead of obstacles. As skeptical as she had been about placing a crystal here, putting a plant there, painting a wall, and rearranging furniture to create a better flow in her environment and consequently her life, she was beginning to think there was something to it. For the first time since she couldn't remember when, there was movement beneath the surface of her everyday life. A stirring in her spirit. A belief that her life could change, and for the better.

She thought Bruno was asleep beside her until she felt his finger trace the length of her spine. It was the second time this week he'd stayed over. Recently cast in an original off-Broadway production, last night he pulled the script from his backpack and diligently highlighted his lines. Similar to Rodin, his world was colorful, passionate, and purposeful, but unlike Rodin, Bruno made her feel like she was always welcome. While he highlighted lines, she had opened her notebook and wrote.

The moment we're in together is right. I don't need him, not in that addictive way. I'm not thinking about him every minute of the day. But when I'm with him I'm relaxed, and I don't worry about being enough. For the first time I'm with a man who doesn't withhold his feelings. I wasted so much time entangled with people who couldn't admit what they felt or wanted. I couldn't even admit what I felt and wanted. I'm done with all of that. I'm done hiding behind or hoping for a man because I've been too afraid to be myself and invest in my own life. Yes, I am done with all of that.

She put her pen down and picked up her guitar. Bruno had spent the evening practicing his lines and she spent it writing a song, each of them absorbed in their own worlds yet occupying the same space.

He tickled the base of her neck with his fingers, and she turned to face him. She tried not to think too deeply about what they were. She liked being with him, and the sex, and that was enough for now.

His eyes were always inquisitive, always searching hers to see how she was. He moved his finger across her collar bone to her shoulder. "Would you like to join me and some actor friends at my place for Thanksgiving? I can't promise the food will be stellar, but the entertainment will be."

"Didn't I tell you I was going to Montana?"

"I thought you might change your mind. Do you really want to go somewhere that is colder than here?" It made her laugh how blatantly he pushed his own agenda.

"I'm not backing out on my best friend."

He frowned. "Of course not, but how will I survive a week without you?" She brushed the hair from his face. He couldn't

The Heart Line

be so attached after two and a half weeks or maybe he was just that needy, although she didn't want to think about him like that. They were having fun, any day with Bruno was light and airy. Which wasn't to say he didn't have substance, only that he was an optimist and didn't preoccupy himself with the shortcomings of the world.

"You'll survive just fine."

"That's what you think." His eyes deadpanned and she couldn't tell what he was going to do until he dug his sharp straight nose under her ear and started to tickle her with his breath and kisses. A high-pitched laugh came out of her as she craned her neck away. Then he rolled on top of her, placed more kisses on her neck and then her breasts. Under the covers he kissed her navel, she opened her legs and felt the warmth of his tongue. He made it so easy to let go.

Eighteen

Shoulders bumped against Bruno as he stepped off the subway at West Fourth Street. The crowds moved toward the stairs and exit with a repressed panic like they sensed the earth above might collapse at any moment. He was too preoccupied by his thoughts of Kay to keep up. *Delightful. Absolutely delightful.* They'd been lying in her bed this morning, her alarm blaring at them to wake up at an ungodly hour because she had the abhorrent responsibility of a nine-to-five job. He'd been hoping to wake up to the orgasmic orchestra she'd complained to him about, but no such luck. She'd pressed the snooze button and hooked her leg around his torso, the weight and soft bristle of it filled him with a refreshing confidence. Half awake, he asked her what he had meant to ask her the night before: Who are your favorite English actors? He asked this for the purely narcissistic purpose of seeing how he measured up, which was an awful idea since he had no major commercial success to measure against. Her eyes were closed. She pressed her lips together as if to warm them up before she spoke. She gave some oldies but goodies: Anthony Hopkins and Michael Caine. He asked about actors his own age. She hummed. "Colin Firth." *Everyone loves Mr. Darcy.* He was definitely respectable, but

The Heart Line

Colin Firth was at least fifteen years older than Bruno. "How old do you think I am?" he asked, his voice betraying a trace of defensiveness. She shrugged, indifferent to his vanity. Then she said, "Jude Law and Paul Bettany." His confidence dropped a notch. He'd set it up that way, what else could be the result of such an inquiry? He couldn't count how many parts he had lost to Jude and Paul, not that he ever had a chance against them; he was simply a pawn in the casting game. "What about Clive Owen?" he asked because Clive was a different type altogether, dark and brooding. He wished he had more of that himself.

She didn't skip a beat, "Too much man."

"Excuse me?"

She lifted her head to look at him. "Have you ever seen *Closer*?" she asked. He nodded, of course he had. He'd seen all Clive's films multiple times. "Well," she continued, as she lowered her head and lazily drew little curlicues on his chest, her level of comfort surprising him considering how reserved she had been when they'd first met three weeks ago, "if you saw him in *Closer*, then that's it."

"What is so apparent to you is totally opaque to me. You're going to have to explain."

She took a deep breath. He was amused by how obvious she thought her point was.

"He was totally Cro-Magnon," she said. "So übermasculine he had enough testosterone for ten men. No restraint. I don't think anybody else could have played it the way he did. It was frightening how convincing he was. Every impulse traveled from his dick to his mouth."

He shook with laughter and she looked at him kind of sheepishly, scrunching her head down into her neck and shoulders like a turtle trying to hide. "I usually don't say things like that."

"Oh, well, you've gone and done it now. You bad, bad girl."

He was laughing to himself in the subway just thinking about it. Too. Much. Man. She obviously liked more effeminate men like himself. This bolstered his confidence, although he wondered if it should be having the opposite effect. He could never compete with the likes of Clive Owen, and now he didn't have to, not that they even remotely occupied the same reality, but one could dream. She probably hadn't seen *Children of Men*; if she saw that she'd change her opinion about Clive. At the top of the stairs a young man, very nicely dressed, maybe a Juilliard student, played the violin with his eyes closed, his movement an ocean storm. Bruno put a couple of dollars in the open case, stepped out onto West Fourth and headed toward the river.

The beginning was always the best, that deep feeling of fascination with an unknown entity staring back at you, reflecting all the wonderful you ever imagined yourself to be. After that chance meeting in the park, he thought he'd never see her again; she was so skeptical of his intentions. He sensed she was somewhat lost and seeking and had wanted to tell her he could be of help, but he didn't say that, too condescending. Thank god he didn't say it because not even a week later, lovely, curious, insecure, and yet determined, she arrived on his doorstep with every intention of sleeping with him. It felt like nothing short of a miracle that he ended up with exactly what he wanted.

He wrapped his coat tightly around him and took a left onto Bleecker Street. He loved this part of town. The streets were wide, and the water was only blocks away, blowing chilled but welcome gusts of wind his way. He made it to Christopher Street to the enormous brick building housing all its secret cells inside, one of them the rehearsal space for his upcoming production. Theater was his home. As much as he craved fame, he loved the community of theater, the unpredictability of live performance, and giving himself over to the moment completely to be left with only the imprint of its memory.

It was time to focus. Before he entered the building, he brought Kay's face to mind one more time. He knew how to enjoy the moment and hoped this would last awhile. He couldn't think beyond "awhile" because it immediately triggered his fear of compromise and habitual security, which were the closest thing to a living death he could imagine. Romance, on the other hand, was fantastic.

Nineteen

Dear Kay,
I'm not writing to defend myself, only to explain. Yes, I had a girlfriend. We'd been together over five years and had even moved in together with plans to marry. You were completely unexpected and so were my feelings for you. I tried to keep a distance from you in hopes that they would pass. They didn't. I couldn't shake you from my mind. When I came looking for you, I rationalized my behavior. I told myself the right time would present itself for me to tell you about my situation. I know, the right time was from that first lunch. I thought you wouldn't give me a chance and walk away, and in the end, you had to anyway. I'm sorry. I hope I haven't done irreparable harm, and that there is a way to regain your confidence, if you'll let me.
Yours,
Peter

She read the email over and over again. He was sincere. Three weeks had passed since she'd left him standing in her office and she was leaving for Montana in two days. As she stood at her bed putting away her laundered clothes, she considered his situation. It was complicated and she could even sympathize. But there was the nagging detail that he'd lacked the courage to be truthful. How could she overlook that?

It took her way too long to really see Rodin. And Peter, well, he had revealed something about himself and wouldn't it be naïve if she just ignored it? She also knew life wasn't always so black and white; maybe he learned from his mistake, and maybe she was being too unforgiving, considering how complicated his situation was. An ache bloomed in her chest. He still wanted a chance, and she wasn't sure she wanted to give him one. It was too much to think about. Given that he'd taken so long to reach out, she certainly didn't feel any pressure to get back to him right away. For weeks she'd been sifting through the chaos of her emotions; they were finally beginning to separate and settle, and then he sends this email. A resolve took hold of her: She wasn't going to let him disrupt her vacation.

Two days later she caught the A line to JFK (the cheapest and, unfortunately, longest way to get there) and was pleasantly surprised to find an entire car empty and her choice of seats, until the doors shut, and the smell hit her. Never had there been a stench so foul. She had no idea how the bowels of the sewer had wafted into this car. Then she saw him in the corner: a man who looked like madness, his matted hair raised on the top of his head like lightning might strike, his skin and clothes invisible beneath a layer of filth, his nails so long they looked like extra appendages. He teetered on the edges of his bare feet, a crooked smile on his face. She gagged and held her breath until she had to take another one. He inched toward her and a panic began to rise in her. *Please, God, oh please, don't let him come any closer, please get me off of this train. Please help him but help me get off this train first.*

He made it to the middle of the car. He laughed to himself and she leaned on the doors in terror until the train pulled into the next stop. The doors slid open, and she bolted, dragging her suitcase behind her and into the next car where she hurriedly sat down next to a woman who seemed to acknowledge Kay's presence by pressing her glasses to her nose while she studiously worked on the NYT crossword puzzle. Never ever would she get on an empty subway car again. She melted into her seat, her heart still racing and her body shuddering as the train rumbled and rattled over the track.

The train took even longer to get to JFK than she'd accounted for and the security line was as fast moving as a line at Disneyland. As soon as she crossed the threshold she sprinted to the gate—an exercise she hadn't undertaken since her high school track days—the bulk of her suitcase obstructed her speed. The heaviness in her legs, the slight taste of blood in her gums, and how swiftly she ran out of breath alarmed her. Maybe she should consider a gym membership when she returned. The last person to board, the agent told her she was lucky, a minute later and the doors would have been shut. A hot mess, she squeezed herself and her suitcase down the aisle. The sweat dripped from her temples as she smiled apologetically at those disapproving passengers annoyed by her tardiness. Her mind and body were in disarray and this was not how she wanted to begin her vacation. At least she had a window seat where she could focus her attention outside. There were few things more soothing than watching the busy world get smaller and smaller and then disappear, replaced by big, billowy clouds. *Good-bye, New York.*

In Bozeman, she picked up her rental car and headed west on the interstate. On her drive to Pony, despite her best efforts, her thoughts drifted to Peter. How he unearthed an energy in her, and how his withholding the truth about his girlfriend struck the latent grief she carried for so many years about her family. A grief that privately wedged itself between her and all her romantic relationships. A grief she thought a healthy romantic relationship would take care of for her. She wondered what exactly had attracted her to Peter in the first place. Where did the chemistry come from? He was so conventional compared to people she'd dated in the past; his life tied to the straight and narrow ladder that led to the top of Preeny. Still, he'd ignited something in her imagination, some kind of potential that she couldn't see but felt deeply. His competence and the way he engaged her with a subtle but visible enthusiasm made her open up to him. There was a tenderness in him, a gentleness that made her feel safe. She didn't really know what was underneath his surface, and she'd probably never find out.

Peter, Bruno, her parents, Preeny, and all the big questions of her life—Was it even possible for her to make a life in New York? Was it possible to shake off the trauma and resentment from her childhood? How long was she going to relive it? Did she have any kind of purpose or destiny? If she left Preeny, what would she do? —loomed over her. Maybe she should go back to California. It was easier there. The pressure to succeed cushioned by the reality that if you didn't succeed you could set up a tent near Zuma Beach and you'd be fine. In New York, you die in the cold. It was a fruitless exercise to think in such extremes. She shook her head and then pushed all these thoughts into a room with a small door where she watched herself take a key and lock it. She shifted her focus to the scenery. The mountains touched the cool blue sky, and a patchwork of snow and yellow earth unfolded like a carpet in front of her. It was difficult to get her bearings. She followed the road and felt lost even though she knew she was headed in the right direction. Maddy called it the middle of nowhere, and Kay could see why, but it also seemed like the place people referred to as God's country—so stark and beautiful, so pristine and natural, you could hear the quiet and couldn't deny your place in the world was a very small one.

Pony itself was smaller than a small town. She saw maybe ten homes driving in. It was quaint, nestled at the base of the Tobacco Root Mountains. A picture-perfect postcard with a main street that had about six storefronts. It looked like (and probably was) a pioneering town from the early nineteenth century. But to live here? Even if it was "God's country," how had Maddy moved from Los Angeles to this place and not lost her mind? No wonder she called Kay as often as she did—what else was there to do?

About a half mile from the center of town she turned down a gravel driveway toward a large modern wood cabin with a green aluminum roof and a wide front porch, where Maddy stood with a blanket around her shoulders.

"Welcome to the great frontier!" shouted Maddy as she flew down the steps and embraced Kay before she'd fully exited the car, nearly knocking Kay off of her feet. "I've been pacing all over the place waiting for you." It had been over a year since they'd seen each other. Too long. "You're pregnant!" said Kay and reached for Maddy's round belly. "You're funny," said Maddy as she pushed the blanket behind her back and turned to model her curvy silhouette. "What do you think?"

"Botticelli. You're a Botticelli." And she was, she had the golden glow, that touch of Venus about her.

They spent the evening with Casey and his parents, eating lasagna and salad and fruit cobbler. Lori and John Caster, Casey's parents, wore flannel shirts and jeans. They could have modeled for an L.L.Bean catalog. They were warm and earthy, and kept trying to pile more food on Kay's plate. The whole Caster family, and even Maddy with her budding belly, looked fit and windblown, like they ventured into the wild every day to climb mountains or fight wolves. She wondered if Mrs. Caster even owned a pair of high heels. A seamstress, she made baby clothes and quilts, which she sold online and at farmers markets in some of the bigger towns a few hours from Pony. Mr. Caster and Casey were developing a custom furniture line and worked out of the barn on their property. They were such a self-sufficient clan, and Kay thought that if there was ever an apocalypse this is where she would come.

Casey made everyone hot chocolate before they all gathered in the living room in front of a fire to play Scrabble. Maddy was a genius at Scrabble and highly competitive. She knew all the obscure two and three letter words and capitalized on every square that multiplied her points. Kay was decent, but long ago had given up trying to compete with Maddy. It wasn't that Maddy could never be beaten, but she was a sore loser, and consequently not very fun to be around after she lost. For Kay, it was a game of leisure, she didn't take it seriously; for Maddy, it reflected her self-worth and so the stakes were high. The game ended when Casey placed a *z* on a triple letter square to create *daze*. Kay was confused by Maddy's modest scowl, it was a significant departure from the slur of profanities she was accustomed to hearing on the rare occasion Maddy lost. She wondered if the change was part of a blossoming maturity that came with her pending motherhood. Casey was attuned to Maddy's scowl though. "You can't win every time," he said, and leaned in to give her a consolation kiss. Then he claimed his victory with an uncoordinated dance that made Kay laugh harder than she had in a while. A sliver of envy surfaced. This was a happy family and Maddy had always been part of one and always would be.

That night it snowed and the next day Casey, Maddy, and Kay went cross-country skiing through looming junipers, spruces, and pines. Kay's lungs and muscles burned as she pushed her long, thin skis through the snow. An image would occasionally slip under the door of the locked room and tug her from the natural world—Peter planting kisses all over her face at the Midtown bar, and then Bruno lying next to her, his piercing eyes and silky touch. Was long-term happiness even a remote possibility with either of them? And then she remembered she was supposed to be on vacation. She shook off the futility of the question and drove the memory of those sweet touches away as she watched her skis glide through the powdery white.

The cold nipped at her face. By noon they arrived at their destination: hot springs. Maddy ordered Casey to turn away while she and Kay stripped off their clothes. Once they lowered themselves into the dark pool of water, Maddy gave Casey permission to strip down. "What? I'm going to be the peep show?" He said smiling while he began to peel off each piece of clothing in a rather awkward striptease. When he reached his boxers, Maddy told Kay to close her eyes and she did as she was told. "You're making her miss the grand finale!" Casey laughed.

"Hon," said Maddy, "in this cold there's no way it's going to be grand."

They soaked for an hour. Kay's muscles loosened, the warm water on her body and the cold air on her face enlivened her. The clinging anxiety and rushed pace of the city dissolved in the water. The wide, open, unlimited blue sky welcomed her to relax into the unknown. They picnicked on chicken soup from a thermos Mrs. Caster had packed for them, as well as thick slices of bread with cheese, and oatmeal raisin cookies. They exited the same way they entered: Casey had to close his eyes while Maddy and Kay darted for their towels and hurriedly dried off, and then Casey got out and Kay had to close her eyes again. "It's not fair," said Casey. "You got to see everyone naked." Maddy gave him a kiss, and he seemed satisfied.

A mile from the house an elk appeared between two trees about thirty feet from them and raised its regal head. Kay felt tiny and awestruck in its presence. She didn't dare take a picture for fear it would flee in the second she searched for her camera. Instead, she paused and admired its size and strength, and its absolute confidence standing there in its natural environment. A shiver electrified her entire body.

With no other people around except the three of them, and no other sound but their breath and the steady swishing of the skis as they continued to make long tracks through the untouched snow, she felt like she was in an enchanted land. It was bliss feeling the strength of her own limbs, the depth of her breath and this pristine nature all around her. She didn't care anymore that Cozumel hadn't worked out.

Maddy and Kay stayed up long after Casey and his parents went to bed that night. They sat on the plush shag rug. With their backs against the legs of the couch they watched the fire embers glow. Maddy rubbed her dome shaped belly. Her face was luminescent. Kay couldn't ever see herself living here (except in the case of an apocalypse), although she could now understand its appeal. And if Maddy stayed here, this could become her regular respite from city life.

"It's like *Little House on the Prairie*," she said.

Maddy chuckled. "Only we have running water and electricity."

"Are you going to raise the baby here?"

"At least the first six months, then we might move to Bozeman or Missoula. We need jobs and a community." Maddy glowed but her voice was flat.

"What's wrong?" Kay asked.

"I'm having a baby, Kay. My life has done a complete one-eighty and I'm not ready for it. My plan was to live a few months in Montana, not to settle here. I love Casey, but I wasn't seriously thinking about getting married or raising a family, that was all supposed to come later. This happened and now it feels like the decision has been made without me. I can't help but feel some regret for not signing with a law firm." Worry set into Maddy's face. "My goal was always to have a thriving career, and now I'm having a baby. I never envisioned my life this way, not in this order."

"It's going to be in a different order and it's going to be okay," said Kay, doing her best to sound like she knew what she was talking about. "You're still going to have a career. It's just going to take a little longer. You might end up pleasantly surprised. You've always excelled at everything you do. You're going to excel at this too."

The worried face transformed into a skeptical one. Kay put her arm around her friend.

Adulthood. The complex, demanding part of life that usurped the fantasies of youth with its mountain of responsibility had lodged itself right in front of Maddy. She would be okay. She would fall in love with the baby and willingly make the compromises such love demanded of her, although it didn't mean she wouldn't suffer the loss of the other lives she had imagined for herself. Kay didn't face any of these challenges; she was still fantasizing about dates with men and how to have a mature relationship. She'd never characterize herself as carefree; however, compared to the responsibility parenthood was about to foist on Maddy, her life was carefree.

Before she went to sleep, she sat in an oversize wicker chair in the corner of the guest room with her journal and pen. *A woman. A mother. Love. What if I don't become a mother? What then? Motherhood is one experience of womanhood; it is not everything. Extraordinary love is extraordinary love, it takes many forms.*

Twenty

Tuesday was "turkey-processing day." Kay thought Maddy was kidding when she said Kay would get to pluck turkey feathers because Kay had been kidding when she said she was up for it. Killing the turkey was a task she assumed they'd take care of well before she arrived in Montana. But Maddy wanted to give Kay a life-on-the-farm experience. Kay didn't want to seem unappreciative of the family's efforts to enrich her vacation, even so she'd just as soon stick to crossing-country skiing, hot springs, board games, and evenings by the fire than watch a turkey flail, headless, against its fate. "Hell no," she said to Maddy in the kitchen when Maddy handed her the knife, killing cone, and bucket to take outside.

"I'm not telling you to kill the turkey," said Maddy. "Casey's going to do it. Just take the stuff outside." Kay did as she was told, put on her coat, hat, and gloves, picked up the killing accoutrements and followed Maddy, who carried an industrial size pot, outside. Maddy put the pot under a spigot and turned it on. A chicken-wire enclosure stood about fifty feet from the house; there three turkeys waddled about, their eyes alert and fearful in their red fleshy masks.

The Heart Line

Casey came outside dressed in Carhartt jeans, workman's boots, and a heavily lined denim jacket. He took a table and burner from the shed and set them up. Maddy turned the spigot off, and Casey hefted the pot of water onto the burner. Kay lay down her tools.

"You ready for this?" asked Casey. He gave Kay a mischievous smile, then pulled a cigarette from his back pocket and lit it. He could have been the Marlboro Man.

"Absolutely not ready," said Kay. She looked at Maddy. "You have no issue watching this killing even as you grow life inside of you?"

"Death is a part of life."

Sure, thought Kay, *we all know that*, but she didn't understand why Maddy wanted to embrace death as part of the life cycle until she had to. And this wasn't just a bird dying from old age; Casey was going to slit its throat. As if she sensed Kay wasn't satisfied with her response, Maddy said, "If we're responsible for ending this bird's life then the least we can do is be courageous enough to be with it at its end to honor its sacrifice."

She was having a difficult time digesting this paradigm. Casey shook his head. "You are both making too much of this. It's Thanksgiving. We eat turkey. If we're going to eat turkey, we have to kill it."

She was done arguing. Her toes and fingers were beginning to hurt from the cold. Casey went into the coop and grabbed one of the birds by its legs so that it hung upside down. The coop door slammed shut with a loud slap as he approached the table. Kay held Maddy's hand and watched.

It wasn't the blood draining from its neck into the bucket, nor the panic so evident in the flapping of its enormous wings that bothered Kay; it was the bird's absolute helplessness. It couldn't do a damn thing to save itself. The only thing that could have saved it was their compassion, but they were accustomed to turkey on Thanksgiving, and they weren't going to give that up. Why Maddy had to thrust these sad truths upon Kay was beyond her. Kay wanted the world to be soft, even though her experience often told her otherwise. And to make sure her feet stayed on the solid ground, Maddy never hesitated to show her the sharp edges.

The beating of the bird's wings against the air was the only sound they could hear, until it stopped. Then Casey removed the head. He placed the turkey in the pot of boiling water. Minutes later he took it out and placed its body in a cooler on the table. Maddy and Kay silently approached and, without any direction they removed their gloves and began to pull at the feathers with their hands. A slight tug and they came off the skin. Kay rubbed her hands over its pink and white goose-pimpled flesh, felt the give of its cooling skin. The mantra that marched from under her breath to the bird: thank you, thank you . . .

Once the bird was deplumed, Casey began to remove the innards and Kay excused herself. She walked back inside the house and sat at the kitchen table. Mrs. Caster stood at the counter chopping sweet potatoes and parsnips. When she saw Kay she asked, "Everything okay?" Kay gave a weak smile. Mrs. Caster didn't persist and five minutes later set a cup of tea in front of Kay. "We don't have much trouble killing animals we're going to eat. I know for most people who aren't ranchers or farmers it can be disturbing." Kay nodded slowly. She tasted lemon and lavender in the tea and appreciated how the heat through the mug warmed her hands.

Mrs. Caster went back to chopping vegetables, her back turned toward Kay; she paused and asked, "What do you think about Maddy and Casey having a baby?" She turned her head back to look at Kay, who quickly tried to gather her thoughts. She superimposed the image of a newborn baby over the image of the dead turkey that was still in her mind. "I think it's exciting," she said, a general response that required little thinking and withheld judgement.

"You think Maddy's ready for it?" Mrs. Caster's tone made her uncomfortable. Why was she fishing like this? What did this woman expect her to say? She wondered if Mrs. Caster considered whether her son was ready to be a father? Mrs. Caster kept her back to Kay as she continued to chop vegetables, as if her question was completely casual and she wasn't really interested in an answer. Kay knew better. She stared at her back, while her mind scrambled for a response, until a few moments later Maddy opened the door and walked into the kitchen, letting in the cold. Casey followed behind her with the turkey in his arms. Relief swept over her.

The bird didn't appear so vulnerable in its now store-bought-looking form. Mrs. Caster quickly grabbed a brining bag from a cupboard and Casey placed the turkey inside. Then she quickly added some salt to the bag and was at the fridge pulling out sage, parsley, thyme, and onion. As she put the herbs and onion in the bag with the turkey, she said, "I think it's time you all went to see Jack."

"Jack? Who's Jack?" Kay asked.

Jack was the owner and bartender of the one bar in Pony, affectionately referred to by the locals as the Saloon. It was a twenty-minute walk from the house. Kay, Maddy, and Casey kicked a path through the gravel and snow as the sun descended behind the mountains. A single streetlamp lit the entirety of the downtown area. Hanging above the door of the saloon, which was just like the ones she'd seen in old western films—wood frame, shingles, front porch—was a sign that read *Bar*. The lights were out. Casey shook his head, "He closes up when it's slow. It's always slow though. He sort of runs 'on demand.'" He cupped his hands around his mouth and yelled toward a lighted window above the bar, "Jack! Oh Jack! You have clientele to serve!" A minute later the window lifted and a man with salt-and-pepper hair and a thick mustache stuck his head out. "Casey Caster!" he yelled. "You hardly count as clientele, although I see you've brought your lucky charm, Ms. Magdalena, with you to persuade me to your favor." He tipped his imaginary hat at Maddy. "Without her and whoever this other lovely lady is" (and Kay got a nod as well) "I'd send your ass packin.'" His voice echoed in the empty street.

"We need your help, Jack. Our friend Kay here is from the big city and she's just come down with a severe case of the turkey blues."

"The turkey blues! Why didn't you say so? We can't have that. Ms. Kay, you've come to the right place." He disappeared from the window and like a magician reappeared a second later behind the front door to let them in.

The floor of the saloon creaked as they walked across it; their noses all woke up with the ancient smell of alcohol, syrupy and acidic, that rose up from it. The place felt cavernous with its tall ceilings and sparse furnishings—a couple of round wood tables with chairs where one might play a card game. Besides the liquor lining the shelves, the only things that caught the eye were a jukebox against the back wall and a foosball table on the far side of the room.

Jack didn't even ask what everyone was drinking, with an elfish grin he announced Wild Turkey was the only way to cure the turkey blues, and quickly poured Casey, Kay, and himself the bourbon over ice. He was mindful to give Maddy a seltzer water. It wasn't Kay's drink of choice, but she didn't care, the burn of the alcohol was like a hot snake traveling from her throat to her belly and it felt good.

Maddy went to the jukebox and selected some songs. U2's "Who's Going to Ride Your Wild Horses" came in over the speakers.

Jack put some peanuts and pretzels on the bar. He was less of a bartender and more of a fellow patron the way he downed the bourbon right along with them. Maddy and Casey walked over to the foosball table.

"Do you ride horses, Jack?" Kay asked. Between the song and Montana this seemed a logical question to her.

He gave her an amused look. "Ms. Kay, I do just about everything. I'm the town mechanic, outdoor guide, fireman, and the proprietor of this respectable establishment. You're damn right I ride horses."

"Cheers." She raised her glass to him. He was more passionate than your average person. She figured he was in his late fifties, around her dad's age. Her dad had a kind of retiring spirit though, whether from all the disappointment he'd suffered in life or from his nature was unclear to her. Jack, however, was a comet with sparks flying from his tail, you had to hold on tight because he had worlds to show you and he was in a hurry. People could be so wildly different from one another.

"And today I'm the local apothecary. How are you feeling?" he asked as he poured more bourbon into her glass.

"Better," she said. "I'm thinking less about Casey taking an axe to the turkey's head." She saw the turkey's head sinking into the amber-colored liquor, disintegrating with each sip she took, her mind and body becoming too relaxed to hold the image of its death.

"It's all that city living. It's bad for the soul, disconnects humans from all things natural because, forgive me, killing a bird is natural. Eating meat . . . natural. You'd be hard pressed to find a Montanan upset about killing a turkey."

"Nobody buys a turkey at the store here?"

"Sure they do. But hunting and killing prey is also just a part of life out here. It's not an ethical question. If we're talking ethics, then killing a turkey on a farm is much more humane than sending it to a slaughterhouse to then show up looking pretty at the store."

"So I've heard. I just don't like watching it."

"You know what we need to do?"

"Drink more?"

"We need to sing the blues out of you."

"I'm not really in the mood for a talent show."

He wasn't listening. He lifted a guitar from behind the bar. "Did I tell you I'm also the town minstrel . . . Maddy and Casey, get over here." They obediently left their foosball game and joined Kay and Jack at the bar, taking a seat on either side of them. Jack strummed with gusto. "Kay, you've got to cast the first line and you're competing with U2 so belt it out." Dread spread in her gut. The Wild Turkey hadn't worked its magic deeply enough yet. Did she have to? Yes, one look at Jack and she could see there was no way to get out of it. Here we go, she thought. A deep breath and: "I've got the turkey blues . . . from my head to my shoes . . . A poultry's paltry life is the essence of my strife . . ."

Jack nodded with encouragement and an ear-to-ear grin. "That's good . . ." he kept working on the guitar and then he nudged Maddy and she started in, "City ways have me blind to how country killing is actually kind . . . That turkey lived damn well so on its death let's not dwell." Maddy, always the devil's

The Heart Line

advocate. Then Jack pointed at Casey, who stuck his chest out and didn't hold back. "What's a person to do for a Thanksgiving feast, we all know turkey's the ideal beast . . . You can have mashed potatoes and gravy but without the turkey . . . well, that's just crazy!"

"Everybody!" yelled Jack. "I've got the turkey blues from my head to my shoes . . . I've got the turkey blues from my head to my shoes . . ." Kay closed her eyes and kept singing, "I've got the turkey blues . . ." She found herself feeling better, uplifted by the absurdity of her blues, and grateful to Jack for his boisterous and generous spirit. When his guitar playing stopped all of a sudden, she opened her eyes. Jack, Casey, and Maddy were all looking toward the front door. Kay followed their stares to where a man stood and stared right back at them. In his black overcoat and oxford shoes he clearly wasn't a local. It took her a minute to place him because it seemed too far-fetched that he would be here in this little-known town, so easy to miss in the dark and two thousand miles from New York City.

"Peter?"

His face was as startled as hers. As though he hadn't expected to find her here and singing the blues no less. Yet he came looking for her (there was no other reason he'd be in this town) and you wouldn't travel all this way and not expect to find the person you were looking for. Even after Jack told him, "Come on in. Make yourself comfortable," and wiped down the bar and poured him a drink ("Wild Turkey is the only drink on the menu tonight") he still didn't say anything. And Kay felt imposed upon. What was he doing interrupting her vacation and without a prepared speech? Not one word. The awkwardness impelled her to make introductions—"Maddy this is Peter; Peter, Maddy."

Maddy shook his hand and looked him over carefully like he could be an impostor. "Peter? The Peter?" It was too much to hope for subtlety from Maddy.

"Yes, it's him," Kay said, and she watched Peter's face change three shades of pink. Then it was on to Casey. "Casey, meet Peter. He's a friend from New York City." Casey nearly shook Peter's arm off. It was hard to tell if he was trying to make him feel welcome or if his overzealous handshake was an implied threat.

Then they all waited expectantly for a story or an explanation. Peter looked abashed like he wanted to hide but mustered to say, "That was some impressive singing. I am really sorry I interrupted y'all." For a split second no one breathed. Not only could Kay not believe he was there, but he'd just said *y'all* as if he'd touched down in the south of the country and not the west. He was more nervous than she realized. He seemed to register his error and clenched his teeth in an apologetic smile.

Jack continued to prove himself a gracious host. "Are you kiddin'? We so rarely have the opportunity to host out-of-towners. We're grateful you came." Then he ushered Casey and Maddy back to their foosball game and said he'd referee. They walked away from the bar while Kay and Peter sat staring at each other. Tom Petty came in over the speakers singing, "Into the great wide open . . ."

Peter moved in his coat like it didn't fit him right. "I feel like I'm a grenade that just rolled in and blew up the good time everyone was having."

She wasn't going to argue, he kind of was like that. "What are you doing here? I didn't tell you I was going to be in Pony."

He looked at her guiltily. "You told Amita. I pleaded with her and she took pity on me. Please don't blame her." It was definitely a mark against Amita. She would have to have a word with her when she got back to the City. Now that she thought of it, it was kind of a mark against Peter too.

"But why are you here?" He had to be out of his mind if he thought she was going to invite him to Thanksgiving.

"I didn't hear from you after I sent that email and I thought that was it, you were brushing me off. I thought coming here might be the only way to show you I'm serious . . ."

Getting to Pony was no easy feat; she was equally flattered and appalled. "How did you expect this to go?" she asked. "I don't have the other glass slipper."

He turned pale.

She didn't mean to belittle or reject him, but what audacity to expect to hear from her right away when he had taken three weeks to reach out and then to track her down when he didn't receive a reply.

His body trembled.

And she could see how vulnerable he'd made himself by coming out here, pinning his hopes and feelings on this moment to undo the mistake he'd made. "Look," she said, "I wasn't brushing you off. I needed time to think."

The room sunk a little. Peter lowered his head. Tom Petty sang "A rebel without a clue." When he looked up again, it was with a resigned smile. "Maybe I did think I could be your Prince Charming," he said. "I guess that possibility has long passed." It sounded like a question.

It had passed. What she wanted was a lot more durable than the trappings of a prince and a glass slipper. "Princes are kind of static," she said. His eyes lifted. She didn't know what to do with him, or what she wanted from him, if anything. "How did you know I was at the bar?"

"I didn't. It was the only storefront with a light on."

"Your plan was to drive to Pony and hope you'd find me?"

"I didn't have a lot of time to plan, but I figured with a population of a hundred I had pretty good odds. And here we are."

But now what? she thought. "We barely know each other," she said.

He nodded in agreement. "We barely know each other," he repeated.

She wasn't sure she wanted to get to know him. The attraction she felt for him had lost its urgency. She was on the other side of it, trying to figure out what it had all been about.

"I'm seeing someone," she said.

His face was solemn. "Is it serious?"

She couldn't say. "I just wanted you to know."

"Thank you." His mind raced behind his eyes. "I'm going to drive back to Bozeman tonight. I'm flying to San Francisco tomorrow to spend Thanksgiving with my mom. I was hoping we could go out when we're back in New York. Talk some more."

She could close this door, say no. Yet, it made a difference he'd come all this way. It made it hard to say no. "Okay," she said.

"Yeah?"

"Yeah."

He brightened and leaned in to kiss her on the cheek. "Cheers," he said. Lifting the glass of Wild Turkey still on the bar, he took it down in one swig. He kissed her on the other cheek. "I'll see you soon."

"Drive safe," she said. Then he opened the door, let in a gust of frigid air, and walked back out into the night. Through the picture window, she watched him actually look both ways before he crossed the dark, empty street. He got into an SUV and drove away. That was it? Less than ten minutes in Pony. If

Maddy, Casey, and Jack hadn't been there to verify he had come, she would have thought he was an apparition—all her romantic fantasies materialized in a brilliant figment of her imagination.

Twenty-one

Driving the interstate from Pony to Bozeman made Peter feel like he was underwater on the Argo in search of the Titanic. His headlights and a patch of stars peeking through the indigo clouds were the only lights visible in what was otherwise a cauldron of black. Each movement forward was like driving off a cliff, and then miraculously the road would rise up in front of him. The radio reception was patchy at best. He turned it off, surrounded by the eerie quiet.

She was "seeing someone." That was fast. She had every right to, though that logic didn't stop a primal sense of possession from overtaking him. What was it that made him feel like she belonged to him? The caveman in him? Did she have any idea how hard it was for him to get on a plane and show up in Pony? It wasn't the logistics he found challenging, it was the sheer force of will and courage it took for him to make a heroic gesture, and she looked at him like he was a lunatic. He thought the risks he took by following these feelings he had for her should yield some kind of return; only now he could see there was a very real possibility that the only return he might get for blowing up his life was nothing.

The Heart Line

He'd made the statement loud and clear by coming out here: *I'm not playing games.* It would have been nice if she'd been more impressed than irritated. He hadn't expected her to be so defensive. But she wouldn't be able to deny he knew how to show up. He succeeded insofar as she agreed to go out with him. It was a tenuous connection though, he had to navigate carefully.

He gripped the steering wheel and pressed his foot on the gas. The empty, open roads were made for speeding. He was traveling through a void. He just wanted to get out of this darkness and get to California. And he just wanted her to understand, to let go and to see he was a great guy. Was it really so hard? Then Sarah popped into his mind: the dead look in her eyes when they'd met last week at Penelope's Café (because she didn't want him at the apartment). Tucked into a corner table, an untouched plate of scrambled eggs in front of her, he was trapped under her gaze. Pale and with dark circles under her eyes, she hadn't bothered to put makeup on, which was unlike her. Her usual fierce determination had drained from her face. She had lost all feeling for him. "You wasted my time," she said, flatly. He hadn't meant to. That statement cut him, everything else she said was a blur after that. It hadn't lasted forever. Did that really mean it was a waste of time? Her face was still in his mind when the road suddenly came back into focus because in that split second something dropped from the sky. He didn't have a moment to respond. The deer hit the front grill and instantly the impact sent Peter's head toward the steering wheel then back as if yanked by a noose around his neck.

An explosion: the air bags smothered him as his arms flailed to push them away. He choked for breath.

Screeching. Was it the tires or the deer?

No. He was screaming.

Hollis T. Miller

The vehicle ran off the road. His foot frantically searched for the brake, another yank to the head as he slammed his foot down and jerked to a stop.

He didn't move. His head lay against the side window and the blood throbbed behind his eyes. He did not want to face the moment; he did not want to face any part of his life. If there was a way to escape, he would, because right now it sucked.

Twenty-two

Kay paired up with Maddy and Jack paired up with Casey for a foosball competition. It was the perfect game to get Peter off her mind. There was no time to think, only time to react as the ball made an erratic path between the foosball men. Kay was surprised by how naturally she took to the game. She hadn't played since college and then it had been only a handful of times. *Damn*, she thought, *I'm not bad*, as she spun one of the handles, smacked the ball and in an instant watched it graze one of Casey's men, ricochet off Jack's defender, and land right in the goal. Maddy and Kay jumped wildly.

"Now, not to discredit your skill, Ms. Kay, but that was a lucky shot, so don't go celebrating just yet," said Jack as he took the ball out of the goal box.

"You just think it's luck because you didn't have the skill to block it," said Kay, and gave Jack a wink and smile.

"Listen to that bravado," he said. "I'd say our Wild Turkey has done its business and washed those blues right out of you."

"You're the man, Jack," Casey chimed in.

Jack pushed the ball into the side chute to start the next point. Maddy took a swing at it. A second later a ringing sounded off from behind the bar.

"Hold up," said Jack. He walked over to the bar and picked up an old yellow rotary phone. " Who is it?" he asked. ". . . Okay. How many miles? . . . Where to? . . . Yeah, I'll do it . . . Hold on, let me get a pen . . . okay, go ahead." Jack scribbled on a napkin and shoved it in his pocket. When he hung up the phone, he put both hands flat on the bar and looked up at Maddy, Casey, and Kay. "Party's over," he said. "My services are needed about fifteen miles from here. There's a roadkill accident and I bet you, Ms. Kay, it's that Prince Charmin' of yours gone and fallen off his horse."

"What?" she said.

"Someone hit a deer then drove off the road and now I need to tow the car and the person to Bozeman. Was your man driving a white Toyota RAV4?"

The ground seemed to shake. "I think so."

"Yep, it's him." He took some keys from a drawer and swung them into his hand.

"You're the tow truck guy too?" Kay asked, unable to grasp the multiple identities Jack slipped on and off.

He nodded. "The rental car companies contract my services. It's a good gig. Pays for my truck. But I gotta go. Casey, you and Maddy know how to lock up. You can stay as long as you like." Then he looked at Kay. "You comin'?"

She stood frozen. The air shifted. Her entire trip pivoted and faced a whole new direction. She looked toward Maddy who settled into one of the table chairs and put her feet up on another.

"You don't have to go," said Maddy, "he got himself into this mess. It's not your responsibility." Maddy was always rational, but it didn't mean she was always right.

"I know it's not my responsibility," said Kay, "but I can't just sit here when I know he came all this way to see me and then ends up in an accident because of it." She looked at Jack. "May I have a glass of water?"

He poured four glasses of water. "We could all use a little hydration." He passed the waters out and they all quickly drank them down, then Kay lifted her coat from the hook by the front door.

"Don't wait up," she said and followed Jack through the back, where there was a large gravel parking lot, his truck the only vehicle in it. He started it up and turned on the heat. Kay hopped inside while he hitched a car dolly to the back. When he got into the truck, Kay asked if he was okay to drive. He chuckled to himself. "Ms. Kay," he said, "three shots of Wild Turkey barely make me blink. You're safe. Don't worry." They were off, heading out into the night, hushed as they listened to the creaking sounds of the dolly in the back and the rush of the road underneath them.

A half hour later the lights of the truck settled like a spotlight on the white RAV4 about twenty-five feet from the road. "There's your man," said Jack.

"He's not my man," Kay snapped. "Sorry."

"Whatever you say, Ms. Kay." He pulled up right in front of the car. The front grill was missing, the bumper smashed in, and a headlight broken. Jack took a flashlight from the glove compartment and got out of the truck. He walked over to the driver's side of the car and Kay followed right behind him. He pointed the flashlight into the side window and consequently right into Peter's eyes; Peter's face retreated like a shocked animal. Jack opened the door, and Peter, enveloped by the sad airbags, looked terrified. He squinted at Jack, who kept the flashlight pointed at Peter's face until he finally said, "You're the guy from Pony."

"That's me," said Jack, taking a closer look at him. "You sure did hit that deer hard. Looks like your nose is broken and you got a nice bump above your left eye."

Peter saw Kay and he looked mystified. "What are you all doing here?"

"You called the rental car company, right?" said Jack.

Peter's head moved slightly.

"As big as Montana is, it's also a very small world. They called me to come get you. How's your neck?"

"Sore," said Peter and gripped it with his left hand.

"Step out of the truck," said Jack.

Peter did as he was told.

Jack continued to shine the flashlight on Peter. "Now I want your eyes to follow my finger . . . good . . . okay. Now, lift one leg at a time . . . How do they feel?"

"Fine."

"Raise your arms up. All the way above your head. Now turn your head to the left—"

"I can't. My neck hurts."

"Anything else hurt?"

"No."

"I'd say whiplash and a broken nose, but you're going to be okay," said Jack. "You want me to reset that nose for you?"

Peter looked at him, slightly horrified. "It's the second time I've broken it. I think it's best if I wait to go to a doctor."

"Suit yourself," said Jack. Then he lifted his head and circled it around like a periscope. "Now, where is that beast? You and Ms. Kay get in the truck and get warm, and I'll get to my business."

From the truck Kay and Peter watched Jack cross the road and disappear into the dark, the floating light from his flashlight the only indicator to identify where he was.

The Heart Line

"You didn't have to come out here," said Peter.

Kay was still looking out the window toward Jack's flashlight bobbing up and down. "I know," she said.

"Why did you?" he asked.

She turned toward him. "I wanted to make sure you were all right." The area around his nose and eyes was swollen. "Are you all right?" she asked.

He took a moment. "You coming to check on me helps. Thank you," he said.

"You're welcome."

The driver's-side door opened, and Jack hopped inside. He drove forward then set the truck in reverse to line it up with the rental. The high-pitched reverse signal sounded as he backed up. Looking through the rear window, he said, "It was a buck. Some pretty big antlers too. He's dead though, so we can be grateful for that."

"What would you have done if he wasn't dead?" asked Peter.

"Put him out of his misery," said Jack.

Peter put his face in his hands.

"Aw, don't take it so hard," said Jack, "hitting deer is as common as tripping over rocks out here." Then he was out of the truck again.

By the time he had the car hooked up to the dolly and returned to the truck it was almost 11:00 p.m. Peter asked him for the flashlight, then got out and walked across the road. The frozen soil crunched beneath his shoes, which felt like they might slip from under him at any moment. The deer seemed small compared to its antlers. They looked like the naked branches of a majestic old tree. He couldn't see any blood. In fact, the buck looked peaceful. It was like the spirit got knocked out of him on impact and who knows where it went. It didn't make Peter feel any better though. He stood shining the light down on the animal for a minute or so. Before he turned around, he said, "I'm sorry."

In the truck, Jack and Kay rubbed their arm sleeves furiously against the fogged-up windows. When Peter got in, Kay moved toward the middle of the seat. Jack maneuvered the truck with its heavy load back onto the road and headed east.

The road was a long dark tunnel. The wind whistled and rattled through all the parts of the truck. Jack leaned his forearms on the steering wheel, his mind focused on the road and then up at the sky where the clouds began to clear and the stars to reveal their brilliance. The cab was warm, and no one said anything for a good long while until Jack broke the silence. "How long have you two known each other?"

Kay and Peter exchanged a glance, both hesitant to answer for fear he was trying to lead them somewhere they didn't want to go. Kay answered, "Not long."

Jack pressed his lips together. "Forces are funny, aren't they?" he said, "There's always the initial impact and then there's whatever we decide to do after that. Do we run from them? Go deeper? You know, ask the hard questions we'd rather avoid."

It was quiet again. "I don't understand what you're trying to say," said Kay.

"There are forces at work tonight. You can't feel them? Some of them are just plain obvious, like that buck. They're not working on me so much as they're working on you two. The both of you have been stripped down. This guy seems to have it a bit harder at the moment though . . ."

"My name's Peter."

"Okay," said Jack. "Well, just remember forces are gods, and they're not playing around." Jack said this very matter-of-factly, as though it made perfect sense. It clearly unnerved Peter, who bit at his thumbnail while worry ran all over his face.

Kay thought some clarity would help. "These forces," she said, "you just mean to pay attention and take them seriously."

Jack puckered his lips toward the roof of the car and thought about it a moment. "I mean you're either going to fuck up or be fucked until you wake up. Pardon my French."

No one said another word until they arrived in Bozeman.

They pulled in just after midnight. Jack stopped at a twenty-four-hour CVS, bought some ibuprofen and a bottle of water, and handed them to Peter. Then they headed to the airport, pulled up curbside, and Jack looked at Peter. "You'll meet Patty at the rental counter. She'll have an accident report for you to fill out." He pulled the napkin he'd written on earlier from his pocket and handed it to Peter. "That's your claim number there. And make sure you get yourself to a doctor tomorrow. I'm going to drop this car off at the autobody."

"Thank you," said Peter. His shoulders and head hung low.

"Don't mention it," said Jack, then he looked at Kay. "I'll give you two a minute."

Kay and Peter stood on the sidewalk in front of the sliding doors that led into the airport. The wind made the cold even colder. Both of them were at a loss for words as they tried to wrap their minds around the last few hours. An energy seemed to take shape and move between them.

"I'm sorry for creating such a mess," said Peter.

"It was an accident," said Kay.

"I'm still sorry," he said. She stepped forward and embraced him. He hugged her back and they stood like that for a while.

"Happy Thanksgiving," she said as she stepped back.

His smile was both pain and gratitude, "Happy Thanksgiving."

Twenty-three

Kay sipped on a grapefruit mimosa while Bruno prepared a frittata. Bacon sizzled in the pan as he diced shallots and sliced broccoli florets. The sweet smell of corn bread wafted from the oven and began to mix with the savory scents in the kitchen. Kay decided the kitchen was her favorite room in the house, especially when Bruno cooked. His absolute focus on the task at hand was oddly pleasurable to observe. His mind gauged the timing of the food; his nose and eyes assessed its flavor. All of his senses were on alert.

"Here," he said, handing her a carton of eggs and a bowl. "Would you please scramble six eggs?"

"Of course." She cracked the eggs one by one into the ceramic blue bowl and whisked a fork through them.

He picked up a pair of tongs and placed the bacon onto a paper towel, then he wiped the skillet clean, added a bit of oil, and threw the shallots and broccoli in.

"Eggs?"

She handed him the bowl.

His hands and arms moved like an orchestra conductor's: he lifted the bowl high and then low and then high again. The eggs stretched and dropped into the pan where they sizzled. He chopped the bacon, sprinkled it on top along with some cheddar, salt, and pepper, and then placed the skillet in the oven. Five minutes later brunch was served.

Lucky sat and whined, desperate for a piece of bacon, and Bruno indulged him. Before he sunk his fork into his food, he looked at Kay. "I missed you," he said.

"That's nice to hear," she said, and it was. His natural warmth and expressiveness made her feel wanted and safe.

"Tell me about your trip."

What to tell, she thought. Jack was one of the highlights, she wasn't sure why except that he was the liveliest character she'd ever met, so she told Bruno about him and his many talents. Bruno nodded as if he was familiar with characters like Jack and said, "He would have been a great actor." She shared the things that made an impression on her: the elk, the turkey, the calm self-sufficiency that living so close to nature instilled in people and how the remoteness of the town sometimes made her feel like she was visiting another planet. It was a respite from city life, but she confessed that by the end of it, she ended up missing the busyness of New York. Being part of its multitude made her feel alive in a completely different way. In Pony, one could just be, but in the City, there was a loud driving call to create, to take action, being wasn't as easy to come by. She figured both being and creating were essential, finding a way to balance these states in any environment was the challenge.

"Hmm," said Bruno, drinking his mimosa. "It sounds like it was an illuminating trip. What would you say we're doing right now, are we being or are we creating?"

"I think we're being," she said.

"And I think we're being and creating, although the creating part is more subtle."

"You mean we're creating something between us?"

"A relationship," he said with authority.

Shyness, tight and warm, slipped over her like a glove. He always cut through the haze, the answers to him were so clear, pure and simple, but nothing ever felt pure and simple to her. He was holding her hand through unfamiliar territory and lighting a path she couldn't see on her own. Wary of imagining anything beyond the moment for fear she'd only end up disenchanted, she hadn't thought about how the moments add up, either they build something or reveal its faults.

"You're blushing," he said.

"I do that sometimes."

"Anything else about your trip?"

Images of Peter and the whole incident that unfolded in Pony passed through her mind and appeared, contemplative and pensive, on her face and Bruno saw it.

"What happened?" he said, a note of suspicion in his voice.

"Nothing."

He chewed on a bite of frittata and tilted his head toward her. "You're not telling me something."

"Your eyes are so intense," she said.

"They help me burrow to the truth."

It didn't seem fair to withhold anything from him. *To tell or not to tell*, she thought. What purpose did withholding serve? Equally, what did it serve to tell him everything? How was Peter relevant to what was going on between her and Bruno?

"Do you remember that 'stuff' I spoke of a while back?"

"Y-es." He waited.

"It kind of showed up in Pony."

"What showed up in Pony?"

"That stuff."

"You're going to have to be more specific."

"A man."

The Heart Line

"Your boyfriend!" His face lit up with an ah-ha look like he'd expected she had a boyfriend all along.

"No! I wouldn't have a boyfriend and be sleeping with you. That's not my way."

"Glad to hear it, but it's not as if it doesn't happen . . . Who is this man? This stuff?"

"Someone I went on two dates with."

"Bloody hell! Two dates and he shows up in Pony?"

"May I have another mimosa?" She shouldn't have mentioned Peter. Bruno got the champagne and grapefruit juice from the refrigerator. He kept his eyes on her while he poured.

"What am I supposed to do?" he said.

"Nothing."

"Well that's just brilliant. He shows up in Pony and I do nothing . . . Why did you tell me this?"

"Because you burrowed those eyes into me, and it seemed pointless to lie about it."

"You shouldn't have told me. I don't know how to compete with that extravagance."

She smiled. "You made a frittata."

"Pffft!" A gush of air burst from his lips. "Well, that makes me feel much better."

"Please," she said, "you don't have to compete."

"Are you joking? This man has laid down the gauntlet. Does he know about me?" He handed her the drink and sat down again.

"I told him I was seeing someone."

"That's something." He took another two bites of frittata, then shoved a piece of corn bread in his mouth and washed it all down with mimosa. He was worried and she regretted bringing it up. His usual ease and cheer was replaced with anxiety. Before he even finished chewing his food, he opened his mouth, "I don't want to know about men who are pursuing you. I'm sure there are many and unless you decide you'd prefer to be with one of them, I'd rather be ignorant of their existence. It'll just keep me up at night."

Lucky let out a high-pitched yelp. In tune with the tension that had quickly taken the air out of the room, the dog cocked its head one way and then another, back and forth like he was trying to decipher the problem.

"I didn't mean to upset you," she said.

He ran his fingers through his hair. "All right, he's not your boyfriend. What is he to you then?"

What could she say? She really didn't know, and she didn't want to lie so she just looked at him, shook her head slightly and said nothing.

He threw his hands up. "Fantastic."

She didn't know what Bruno was to her either. It seemed premature to define these relationships because in both cases there wasn't enough there yet to define.

Bruno's vulnerability was endearing. The competitive urge was so primal, it was foolish of her to think he could be objective about Peter. Maybe she wanted to see his response, to know his natural instinct was to fight for her. Or was it a destructive impulse, her not so subtle manipulation undermining her desire for a relationship? Underneath her deep need for love there was a deeper fear that she might not be capable of it nor able to recognize or receive it if it came into her life. She could only hope love was somewhere down the line.

She went home after breakfast. It wasn't hard to make an excuse. She'd only returned the day before. She was tired and still needed to unpack.

At home she relaxed on her couch. *I want my own life. A life I can look at and say I participated in. A life where I am not on the sidelines always observing, always feeling smaller and less than others. My worth doesn't depend on someone else's approval of me. I don't owe Peter or Bruno anything except the truth. I'm going to stay in New York. There is more possibility for change here. This city is always transforming, renewing itself. I'm going to follow its lead. I make my own living. I have my own apartment. I have interests and passions to explore. I am going to give myself a chance here. I am just beginning.*

Twenty-four

The studio was on the top floor of a brick town house on the Upper West Side. The landlord, an older man, with a chubby middle and thin face wheezed as he opened the door to the apartment and told Peter to take his time, he'd wait downstairs for him. Peter hoped the man wouldn't have a heart attack on the way down. The room was clean and bright and five hundred square feet. Afternoon light poured through the two windows facing the street. Behind him, just left of the front door, was a built-in bookcase. Crown molding framed the ceiling, and baseboards lined the polished wood floors, which creaked as he crossed them to the kitchen: a white porcelain sink, stove, five white cupboards, and a marble countertop along the right wall.

Sarah had agreed to give him the bed in exchange for the couch. It was a fair trade, although looking at this space he wasn't so sure he wanted a bed that would occupy almost half of the room; a couch bed would be a better option, or a bigger space. He had already looked at a number of one-bedrooms, most of them sleek and modern with all the allure of modern amenities: gym, doorman, communal outdoor space with a firepit and grill, views. This, however, was the first space that felt warm and private. It was located in the middle of the block on a tree-lined street, and he immediately noticed the calm. Unlike the other properties he had seen, it reminded him less of a hotel and more of a home. There wasn't a doorman, nor was there an elevator, but he didn't care. It just felt right. He signed the lease the next morning.

Home.

As if the accident in Pony wasn't enough to unmoor Peter, his father showed up for two nights over Thanksgiving while he was in California. Peter hadn't prepared himself. Over the years, the burden of care had become too much for his mom; she made the only decision she felt she could and placed her husband at Gateway, a nursing home for stroke patients. From the living room bay window of his childhood home, Peter watched the white van with *Gateway* in green script on its side pull up to the curb. An attendant stepped out, glanced at his clipboard in one hand, opened the sliding door with the other, and pressed a button inside the van. The wheelchair lift dropped open and there was his dad.

His dad had suffered three more strokes since Peter had moved to the East Coast, and probably a dozen that had gone undetected. The right side of his face slack, a tremor in both hands, many of the words that fell from his mouth were shapeless; all one could do was acknowledge the sounds with a gentle, understanding nod. Peter continued to watch as the attendant released the brakes on the wheelchair and pushed his dad up the recently installed side ramp to the house. The one thing that put Peter at ease was seeing his dad dressed nicely in khaki pants, a long-sleeve polo shirt, and brown leather sneakers. His hair, pure silver now, was cut neat and short, and he was clean-shaven. It was unlike the image he had carried with him for years of his dad in a frayed terry-cloth robe with disheveled hair and a patchy unkempt beard. Peter's mom, Cathy, insisted that the staff at Gateway made sure her husband, Leland, dressed every day and not linger listless in his robe like other clients she'd seen. Every week she brought him clean pressed clothes and every six weeks she took him on an outing to the barber.

When the attendant was steps away from the door, Peter started to call out to his mom who was in the kitchen prepping food, until he stopped himself. He took a deep breath and held it for a minute before he opened the door.

He said hello to the attendant and then bent to his knees to get eye-level with his father. "Hiya, Dad. How are you?"

Leland's right eye popped wide open when he saw Peter. He wasn't sure if his dad was surprised to see him or if the bruises under both of his eyes had caught him off guard. Half of Leland's face turned up in a brilliant smile. "Gooh," he said "appy," his voice was lively and cheerful. He lifted a shaky arm over Peter's shoulder and Peter came in for an awkward, much needed hug.

Four years since he'd come home for a holiday, he'd forgotten what it was like to be surrounded by family. His grandparents on both sides had passed but Uncle Ron, his dad's brother, showed up with Lily and Jocelyn, his two cousins who were now young women in college, no longer the giggly, squirmy girls who'd annoyed him so long ago. His mom's sister, Aunt Clara, widowed five years ago, arrived with apple and strawberry rhubarb pie and stories about her online dating experiences. As usual, his mom made the table into an art installation: an off-white linen tablecloth and mustard yellow table runner, with a cornucopia of squash, apples, and wheat at the center and candles interwoven from one end of the table to the other. She never overlooked the importance of beauty and the nurturing affect it had on the soul.

Everyone was overjoyed to see him. Their voices boomed with enthusiasm and interest, as well as concern, as they took in his beat-up face. "You going to tell us what happened?" his Uncle Ron asked, as he shoved a crostini with artichoke dip in his mouth. The comfort and familiarity of home was instant. *Sure, why not*, he thought. So, he told the story of how he traveled to Pony, Montana, to woo the woman of his dreams and how it literally backfired in his face.

His aunt commended him for being romantic and brave. His cousin Jocelyn said she wished someone would do that for her. He wished Kay felt the same way. It was too bad about the deer, they all said. He didn't mention Sarah nor how he hadn't been forthright with Kay—he'd already confessed all of this to his mom when he'd arrived home the day before. Her understanding nod and shocked eyes did enough to stoke his guilt, although that wasn't her intention. A single confession was enough.

The sideboard was populated with a feast of turkey and ham, mashed potatoes and gravy, cranberry sauce, roasted brussels sprouts, creamed spinach, pear and pecan salad, dinner rolls and butter. It was embarrassing how much food there was, but what was Thanksgiving without gluttony. As they sat down to eat, Peter found himself glancing at his father every few seconds. His mom sat at the head of the table and his dad sat to the left of her while she cut his food then handed him his fork, which he was able to use independently. His dad was unexpectedly present. The mobile side of his face responded to conversation with animated gestures and gruff enthusiastic words ("No ay!" "es!"). His father was no longer the shadowy figure lost in the ether of his own mind, as he was after that first stroke. Peter was relieved to see this human side of his father he'd forgotten. The mashed potatoes sank into his chest, along with a deep regret as he thought about how zealously he avoided his father for so many years.

The day after Thanksgiving, his mom asked him to help prepare his father for a shower. She'd had the tub removed and the shower expanded so she could roll a shower chair into it. She pulled Leland's nightshirt over his head and then asked Peter to lift him. Desperate to help his dad, even through his pain and bruises, he put his shoulder under his father's shoulder and hoisted him up on his side while his mom quickly slipped his pants and underwear off. His father's bones protruded beneath his dry, crepey skin. Peter winced as he pivoted with his dad on his side and placed him as carefully as he could in the shower chair, though he still went down with a thump. As he backed away, his dad's hand jerked forward and grabbed the back of Peter's neck; squeezing him at the base of his head, he tugged Peter toward him, "Son," he said, perfectly clear. The single word broke him. It took all his strength to look his dad in the eye and hold his gaze for as long as was bearable. He kissed his dad on the cheek and saw tears stream down his mother's face before he left the room.

The best part of the day was breakfast. He'd bought a two-top round wood table at the Housing Works thrift shop and placed it in front of the long windows of his new apartment. From his breakfast nook, he began the day watching the sun rise and the street come to life. He made a game of identifying his neighbors and gave them fictitious names: Mr. Trumpet lived straight across the street, was always dressed in an undershirt, suspenders, and pale blue slacks, and quite literally, like a rooster waking up the neighborhood, stood in front of his window blowing his horn every morning. No one complained. He played well, and it was more pleasant than the repetitive ding of an alarm clock. After seeing a gaggle of women gathered on his stoop two Sundays in a row, their skirts and dresses peeking from beneath their fine coats as though they were going to church, chattering and cackling like teenagers with secrets, he'd decided they were the Golden Girls. There were Romeo and Juliet. Juliet lived a few houses down on the other side of the street. She looked about fourteen. Nearly every day of the week she sat at the upstairs window waiting for Romeo, who would show up on the street below, backpack on, ready for school. He never rang the doorbell, just looked up, and a minute later she would be at the front door to greet him. He watched them now, all giddy and cheerful as they sat on the stoop, leaned into each other, their hands tenderly exchanging touches as they drank each other in until they rose to their feet, a bit unsteady, and headed off hand in hand to school. As they approached the end of the block and turned left out of sight, a tremor of longing zipped through him. New love. Kay.

The morning scenes on the block were the highlight of Peter's day. It was that little bit of unexpected life that kept him afloat in what he'd self-diagnosed as his quarter-life crisis. He hadn't quit Preeny. Not yet. He needed to figure out what came next, and he wasn't sure how to figure it out because for too many years now he'd been watching his life from the outside like a series of pictures he'd curated; the pictures looked nice, he just wasn't really in them. If it were as simple as stepping into life, he would, but it was messier than that. When you're not really there, when there is a whole world in you that has shut down, how do you deal with the chaos when all of a sudden it turns on? He didn't know, except not to run from it, and he hoped that with some time and attention the chaos would clear, and he'd land.

Twenty-five

Christmas was two weeks away and the City was ablaze, more luminous than its natural state, more luminous than one would ever think possible. Three-dimensional stars glowed behind the glass of the Time Warner Center. Along Fifty-Ninth Street the horses and carriages were dressed and lit for the season. Kay waited at the Columbus Circle entrance to Central Park where traffic whirred round and round, and when a light turned red, waves of people rushed across the streets, their eyes and noses peeping between their scarves and hats.

Her nerves a feathery tickle in her stomach (how was he ever going to find her in these crowds?), she glanced at her phone. Just after five o'clock. The next second, she looked up and there was Peter, standing right in front of her. Both surprised to see each other despite the fact that they'd arranged to meet here at this time. They exchanged a quick hug and hello and decided they needed to move away from the crowds. Bundled in their winter attire, they didn't allow the freezing weather to deter them from a walk in the park. They followed the path north through a colonnade of trees cloaked in white lights.

"How was California?" she asked.

"It was hard. I'm glad I went, though." He paused a moment before he continued, "I hadn't seen my dad for a long time. He's an old man now. His speech is impaired and he's in a wheelchair. But his spirit is stronger than I remember and he's more aware. I avoided him for so long, I never gave myself a chance to really miss him."

She looked at him thoughtfully, "Now you miss him?"

"I do. I want to get to know him again, if I can. I'm going back to visit for Christmas."

"I'm going back to visit my family for Christmas too."

"Really? Who are you going to stay with?"

"I'll split my time between my mom's place and my dad's. I usually stay with my dad. I have a habit of avoiding my mom and I don't want to do that anymore either." Her mom had called her shortly after Thanksgiving posing the question again: Would Kay come for the holidays? And Kay was tired, worn out from holding on so tightly to her grievances she didn't have the strength or will to do it anymore. She considered that her mom had a story too. Perhaps when her mom had left the family her heart broke even as she'd followed it. She told her mom she'd consider Christmas, and when she hung up the phone she reflected back to the time when there was no stronger love than the love she felt for her mother. Then she booked the ticket.

She shook her head lightly. "Family. I used to think I didn't need them."

"I understand," he said.

"I think it's great that you're determined to make your dad more a part of your life."

"Thank you." They walked slowly, a slender reverence occupying the space between them. "It's nice to talk to someone."

"It is," she said and wondered how often he felt lonely.

The Heart Line

He stood a little straighter and took a deep breath. "I want you to know that I'm not living with my girlfriend anymore. We broke up and I'm in my own place now. I know you're involved with someone and I'm trying to figure out my life, but I would like to keep seeing you. I want to be in your life somehow. I want you to be in my life."

He was earnest and she was disarmed by it. She wasn't angry at him anymore, that vanished after the accident in Pony. Before that it had been easier to feel self-righteous, easier than feeling her sadness. "I need a little time. I'm here though because I wanted to see you," she said.

Their eyes met and he smiled gently. They approached Tavern on the Green. It was glittering bright and white, a winter wonderland. They were quiet again, both of them less intoxicated by each other's presence and more comfortable and at ease than when they'd first met. They walked east and then south past Wollman's ice-skating rink. Peter stopped.

"You want to go ice skating?" he asked.

She looked at all the people, a hive of bees busy on the ice. "I want to want to go ice-skating. I just don't have a great sense of balance, as you know," she said.

"You do have an awful sense of balance."

"What!"

"You can't get mad! You said it first. We are both witnesses to your lack of balance."

"You're supposed to say, 'No, you're as graceful as a swan.'"

"Really? I thought we were going to be brutally honest with each other from here on out."

"No, no. Honest, sure. Brutal, no thank you."

"Was I that brutal?"

She shrugged. "I like to think I'm graceful."

"No one's stopping you from thinking it."

She bumped him with her shoulder. "It's not that easy when you don't agree."

He shook his head. "I don't know how to keep up when you say one thing and you mean something else entirely."

"Not exactly. I was just trying to skillfully reject your ice-skating invitation without bluntly saying, 'I don't want to go ice-skating.' I was trying to be polite by pretending my lack of balance was the issue."

"Well, for the record," he stuck his gloved hand in his scarf and itched at his neck, "I find your lack of balance endearing."

"I'm going to try to take that as a compliment."

"You absolutely should," he was grinning ear-to-ear. "I don't really want to go ice-skating either. To be in the cold and then step on ice with razor blades under my feet, I'll fall at least once and likely break a bone, not my idea of a good time."

"So why propose it?"

"We're in Central Park, there's the ice rink, it has a certain je ne sais quoi quality to it. It's hard to break the let's-do-what-everyone-else-says-is-fun habit; however, *watching* people lose their balance is very entertaining."

She couldn't disagree. They stood on the perimeter of the rink and watched people with normally flexible joints become stiff with fear and inexperience, and then plow into each other. "It's kind of like how we met," she said.

"You're right and since we've already met there's no need to do it again. Which reminds me . . ." He held up a small red paper shopping bag, the two handles tied together with silver and gold ribbon. She hadn't noticed it at his side. "Merry Christmas," he said. "Oh, my gosh, you look terrified. Don't worry, it's not an engagement ring, it's not anything you have to commit to."

"Phew," she said and stared at the bag.

The Heart Line

"Are you going to open it?"

She took it, untied the ribbon, sunk her hand into the red tissue paper and pulled out a rectangular box: *I Love Lucy*, the complete box set of DVDs. She was touched by his thoughtfulness and couldn't stop smiling at Lucille Ball on the cover with her look of surprise and unassuming mischief.

"Thank you."

"You're welcome. If you ever want company to watch them with just let me know."

"I will."

His eyes turned soft, and she was afraid he might kiss her. Not that she didn't want him to kiss her, she couldn't deny the familiar passion that stirred in her, but she wanted to enjoy the stirring. Overcomplicating her life could wait. A faint relief surfaced in her when he said, "Hot chocolate?"

"Yes, please."

They walked back toward Fifty-Ninth Street to the Time Warner Center and took the escalator up to Bouchon. People crowded into every visible space, their movement and voices reverberated off the walls like the hum of an engine. Miraculously, they snagged a highboy table right in front of the café. The velvety chocolate slid down her throat.

"Do you go duck hunting often?" she asked.

"Say what?" He put his hand to his head on top of which sat a hunter's hat, long flaps alongside his ears and another flap buttoned above his forehead. "I forgot I had this on." He took it off. "It's the best winter hat I've ever had. Not exactly New York hip, but incredibly practical. I bought it at the Bozeman airport to commemorate that fiasco of a trip."

She nodded. "It was a fiasco, wasn't it?" she said faintly.

"No, not like that. You're here and that was the point."

Heat flooded her face.

"I think we can agree hitting that deer and breaking my nose was the fiasco part. And that Jack guy . . . he completely freaked me out. He was like some character from a David Lynch film."

"You watch David Lynch films?"

He was amused. "You shouldn't be so shocked. I grew up in Northern California and my mother's an artist."

She wasn't sure how these personal facts added up to him liking David Lynch, but she was shocked. They might have more in common than she thought. Her attention shifted to the yellow-purple hue beneath his eyes, uncertain if it was a fading bruise from the accident or the effect of some extremely late nights. As if he read her mind, he placed a finger under each eye. "Yes," he said, "these are the last visible traces of my broken nose."

"Ouch," she said.

"It doesn't hurt anymore. By the way I was admiring your boots while we were walking."

"These are *my* Montana souvenir." She kicked her right leg out, flexing and pointing her foot like a ballerina. "They are very hard to trip in." They were a moccasin-style boot: dark brown suede leather that laced up to just under her knee.

"Very bohemian. Makes me think of Berkeley. I like them."

He wanted to know if she had any New Year's resolutions. "I resolve to do the things that make me happy," she said. "I've signed up for guitar lessons and a cooking class, they both start the end of January. What about you?"

He thought a moment. "I resolve to be a better person."

"That's admirable as well as way too big and vague."

"You're right. I resolve to . . . relax and reflect more. I might explore meditation, and I think I'm going to work on the Obama campaign."

"Really? That's incredibly exciting." David Lynch films. Obama. He was coming in and out of focus. She'd made assumptions about him she hadn't even known she had made until now.

"They're looking for all kinds of help if you want to get involved."

She'd never considered getting involved in politics before; it seemed an impossible game to win with your integrity intact. But Obama, he wiped away cynicism. "Hmm," she said. "I'll think about it."

"The moment is going to go by fast."

"Are you taking a leave of absence, or are you leaving Preeny altogether?" she asked and noted a dull pain in her stomach at the thought of him gone.

"I won't stay at Preeny for the long-term. I still need to figure out the timing of my exit." A feeling that had been floating, ungrounded, settled between them now. They saw each other a little more clearly.

Before they left Time Warner, they went to the top floor and looked out the enormous east-facing window where the City's order became apparent: cars moved neatly east and west in their respective lanes, then spiraled around Columbus and flowed into the flowering veins of the avenues toward their destinations. To the left, Central Park opened the sky for a view of the buildings on its periphery, allowing the City to see itself. It was almost peaceful.

Back outside on the street, they hovered near a column to avoid being submerged in the crowds. "I could walk you to your stop," he said.

"Thanks. I think I'm going to take my time though and walk down to Radio City and take in the sights."

"It's pretty spectacular this time of year," he said. There were those soft eyes again. She could have invited him to go with her, but she wanted to take in the City on her own.

"This was nice," she said.

"I hope we can do it again soon."

"I'd like that."

"Well, happy holidays," he said. In anxious excitement they leaned in for a cheek kiss; his lips pressed the corner of her mouth and her forehead hit his brow bone. They both took an unsteady step back. He pressed the heel of his palm to his forehead. "Ow," he said. "We'll get it right someday."

A guttural laugh broke between them. Tears creeped into the corner of her eyes. It wasn't over. *This may just be the beginning*, she thought. Quickly, she stood on her toes and kissed him with perfect precision on the mouth, her lips lingering there for a moment before she pulled away.

"Happy holidays," she said, then turned and walked toward Fifth Avenue while he stood, beguiled, and watched her go.

She marveled as she made her way down Fifth Avenue. Glistening trees sprouted from the sidewalk. Inside the storefronts, snow shimmered, and sparkling woodland creatures raised their heads to exquisitely costumed mannequins. Layers of tulle filled glittering ballrooms. Holograms of giant snowflakes danced along the sides of buildings to carols that fell from the sky.

People moved swiftly with their shopping bags, colorful and cumbersome, swinging at their sides. Yellow taxicabs like globes of light brightened the sea of dark cars all heading downtown. Optimism pervaded the air, it swirled around her. The City was the most mesmerizing enchantress, a living fairy tale. She could feel the dream of it move within her and the ground beneath her feet as she took it in one step at a time.

Acknowledgements

Without the help and support of family and friends this book likely would have remained on my computer, an eternal work in progress. Thank you to those friends and family who read the book and gave me much needed feedback and encouragement: Ryan, Katie, Kenley, Bailey, Kelly, and Louise. Katie, thank you for undertaking designing the cover. I've always admired your style, and I'm so happy it's showcased on the cover. Ricci W. at Written Word Media, thank you for planting the seed in the first place. And thank you for your friendship and expertise, which have been essential in this process. Nicholas Erik, I'm so grateful for those initial conversations we had to get me oriented. Maria T., for letting me know I needed to cross the bridge, and for standing by and encouraging me until I did, I can't thank you enough. I am forever grateful to my mom and the memory of my dad for inspiring me to live from my creativity. And always, thank you to my husband and daughter for listening patiently, cheering me on, and for teaching me about love every day.

Made in the USA
Las Vegas, NV
16 October 2021